JAGUAR TRANSIT

SciFi Suspense with a Metaphysical Twist

Crystal Ceres Time Travel Books #2

I0549351

DogStar Press

Jaguar Transit
Copyright ©2015 Laure Edwards Reminick
ISBN 978-0-9965264-1-8 PRINT

April 2015

Published and Distributed by DogStar Press
P.O. Box 1793, Fairfield, IA 52556
www.DogStar-Press.com

For my mother, Pat Williams

Profound thanks to Nicole Winning
for her unfailing patience

Chapter 1

The door to the Paris apartment slid open silently. But Alexa remained standing in the hallway, transfixed by the realization that just dawned.

Many months had passed since KAG8 declared it would terrorize and dominate her.

Yet, in all this time, there's been not a single peep from that nutzoid computer—oh, excuse me, artificial intelligence.

Hah. I win.

I stepped inside and the front door closed behind me with a swish, to be enveloped by the serene hush of Pearson's home. Undoubtedly, life with Pearson—my robot lover—was good; all anyone could desire of luxurious living, with no desire unfulfilled.

Except, I'm still here in 2962. Not my century...

Shifting new clothes from one hand to the other, I maneuvered through the formal living room, all the while marveling that the old "epitome of all evil" had lost track of me. Perhaps the thing was simply a crazed collection of zeros and ones, after all. On the subject of KAG8, I had always put up a good front, while working hard to stuff churning anxiety.

At the master bedroom door, however, the sight of my dog curled on a pillow warmed my heart. Truly, Bill the Chihuahua effortlessley trumped any stupid fear. Maybe now I could relax and make a life for myself.

I tiptoed by. Evidently not quietly enough, however, because he raised his head right as I made it into the closet. Immediately, the questions began. "Where have you been?"

"Shopping."

I had to laugh out loud at his response. My dog might be a

machine, but somehow he'd picked up the very Parisian ironic gesture of lifting a single eyebrow.

Years earlier, Pearson created Bill the robotic canine to be unrecognizable from the real thing, just like his "father." Thus, Bill appeared exactly as other dogs, until, of course, he launched on long and involved theories regarding the state of world affairs, or about the cute little girl dog that recently sauntered past.

Opinions of my afternoon's activities aside, Bill pranced across the bed toward me. A quick kiss on his noggin, and I headed toward the office in the opposite wing of the apartment, Bill following along. About halfway across the living room, he peered up at me and asked, "Want to play tug of war?" Trying to keep from being dragged across the carpet by my foot-high dog is a good way to keep in shape.

"How about later?" I offered cheerily. When you're desperate for something to do, even organizing a book collection is a pleasure.

Pearson's library had become totally jumbled. I'd found a book on reincarnation buried in a folder labeled *Mechanics of Space Flight*, and his extensive collection of astrology books had been filed away in the *Fine Literature* folder. Pearson was a well-read robot.

Our path passed the kitchen, where real human ladies were cleaning. Pearson wouldn't allow cleaning robots in his offices, spaceships or homes. And me taking care of the apartment also wasn't part of his plan.

I never interacted with the ladies much, but their chatter in the background had been generally enjoyable, even soothing, the recent months. Since I had returned that day from my hunting-and-gathering activities early and lunch wasn't expected until later, I said nothing to them.

Their conversation spilled into the living room, ultimately

proving the ladies had no idea I was around.

Giselle wondered allowed, "Why has not the Capitaine Pearson become tired of this woman?"

"You are only jealous," said the other lady.

"Oui. The Capitaine is very handsome. If I was his mistress, I would remain faithful. Not like her. You see, two nights ago, I saw her with another man in their bedroom."

I could have responded. But they worked for Pearson, not me.

Besides, Pearson and I kept more than one secret. Very few knew about him being a robot. But that fact also made it possible for him to morph into my fiancé, Mac, every night. In fact, back in about 2012, Mac had specifically given the robot-that-would-evolve-into-Pearson that very ability, in case I wasn't able to travel back through time.

Which I hadn't. Yet.

Someday, perhaps I will return home. Maybe. I hope.

I was about to close the hallway door behind us on the way to the office, but stopped when the front door buzzer sounded. No one ever visited if Pearson wasn't present, and the few people I spoke with—mostly Pearson's employees—knew he'd be gone for days.

We waited in the hallway as a lady hurried to answer the door—the one who'd be happy to take my place. When she noticed my presence, her hand almost made it to her mouth. Eyes wide, she made a brief curtsy in my direction and scurried to the door.

"Hello, is Alexa Jane Alden in?" came a male voice. "If so, would you tell her Zaire Chevalier is here?"

"Oh, oui," said the lady. "Wait a moment, s'il vous plait." No surprise, Giselle was slow to come find me.

But that allowed a moment for me to touch my hairstyle here

and there; corkscrew curls always refuse to stay in place.

Giselle came to a stop in front of me, hands tightly clasped. "Mademoiselle Alden? Someone is at the door for you, a Monsieur Chevalier." She opened her hands wide in supplication. "I am very sorry. I did not know you had returned."

My eyebrows might have risen to one of those haughty ironic places. "I would be delighted to see Mr. Chevalier. Please show him in."

When he entered the living room, Zaire and I gave each other a big hug. He didn't seem to mind that I accidentally pulled one of his dreadlocks from the professional brown band holding them back.

"Unless this is a social call, Zaire, I'm guessing you located Rachel." As I made the statement, it struck me how long it had been since I'd thought of my best girlfriend—the one who went back in time, instead of me.

While easing into one of the chairs, Zaire absentmindedly tucked his dreadlock back into place. "Yeah, found her. For a bit it seemed impossible, despite my best efforts in data mining. Then some anonymous source sent me access codes to three old databases." Zaire reached down to rub behind Bill's ears. "It was strange receiving those codes, and I wouldn't usually trust that type of source. But the data was from exactly the time I needed."

"Tell me, did Rachel have a good life?" As I asked, Bill jumped up onto the sofa beside me and settled against my leg.

"She did, if you define high society that way."

I snorted. Though beautiful, Rachel had never been the type to think much about the social elite.

Rachel and I had caroused together in our small Florida town during and after high school early in the 2000s. We lived a life that could not have prepared us for being wrenched to the planet

Adalans and the current century. Months ago, she and I parted ways in a tiny garden shed beside the River Ganges—on the same beach where I'd left Zaire.

"Photos of her at various events appeared rather haute monde to me." He glanced up. "You see, she married. Maybe she was a trophy spouse."

"Married? Oh good, perhaps to that gallery owner. So, who?"

As Zaire's notepad powered up, he asked, "You want the database information?" After inputting my address he hit send, and then paged through his notes. "Okay, here's the name: Armstrong."

At this, my breath stopped. *No, it couldn't be.*

"Yeah," he said, nodding to himself. "Armstrong MacPhearson, in the Bahamas."

I swear my heart dropped to the other side of the world, and broke when it hit. Stunned, I could only focus on the carpet.

Mac, my fiancé. For Mac, I had braved space pirates and murderous robots in order to return through time to him, and the marriage we planned. And now, it appeared the love of my life had managed to get along just fine without me.

Bill tried to nudge his nose under my hand.

The reporter turned his pad toward me, and I recoiled—though not quick enough to avoid certain details on the photo.

"Thank you, Zaire."

He glanced up in surprise at my tone. "Is something wrong?"

"Thank you for checking in." I stood and headed to the front door. He could hardly not follow along. "But turns out I have an appointment."

"I thought you would tell me the whole story," said Zaire. "You said if I found Rachel you would explain everything, how Rachel could have such a life then, when I knew her now."

With a face that roughly translated into, *How can I explain this?*, I put him off. "It's a very long tale, so I'm afraid we will have to get together another time." Which would be never, if I could help it.

Being a newsman, he parried with, "How about Thursday. I could take you to lunch."

I practically pushed him out the door. "Check in with me later?"

After the whoosh of the door sealing closed, I had a moment of silence. Even Bill said nothing. Alas, the sound of clattering dishes intruded.

"Ladies?" In the kitchen, they turned at my voice. "You can take the rest of the afternoon off." They appeared afraid that I might fire them for gossiping. "It's all right, your jobs are safe." I took a deep breath. "It's simply time for you to leave." They continued to not move. "For today."

Determined to reclaim my space, I lingered nearby. As the ladies finally headed for the apartment's back door, I followed till they nodded to the guard outside and then disappeared from view.

Hard to know how long I stood there, staring at nothing. Eventually, Bill nudged me, and when I picked him up he reached to nuzzle my cheek. After creeping to a wall of windows, I gazed out over the ever-renewed city. The top of the Eiffel Tower was visible over some buildings, because Paris continued to insist that landmark dominate the skyline.

Zaire's photo had betrayed a date only a few months after Rachel found herself in Florida—with strange clues about my disappearance and no memories to match the information. The authorities had declared me dead. Almost immediately, Mac had begun creating the robot that would become Pearson.

Recollections trounced through my heart. Times when Mac and Rachel shared an easy laugh over a joke that I needed an extra moment to understand. *Naïve, just plain naïve.*

Life in Paris with a human-shaped robot playing the role of an ersatz Mac; a sham, an illusion.

The dishwasher switched over to the next cycle. On the mantel, an heirloom clock from the 2700s marked the quarter hour with its intricate beeps.

Bill said, "You are upset. Did you want me to bite his ankle?" He looked up at me quite seriously. I managed a tiny smile at his joke, since we both knew he couldn't hurt a human.

"No, it's okay."

My heart latched onto a possible explanation. The photo appeared to have been taken at a society event. So, perhaps Rachel had simply been a dinner companion and the whole scenario was conjured by an overeager journalist.

I marched into Pearson's office and settled at the desk with Bill on my lap. A data pad was already rolled out flat, and Zaire's list waited for me in my email. Finally, it made sense to make a payment from the account Pearson maintained for such necessities. I zeroed in on my century and my region; available were lists of driver's licenses, voter registrations. I even found documents for Alexa Jane Alden, but there was no reason to linger over my death certificate.

Already in the correct part of the century, Rachel was easy to locate. A snort escaped me at the official record of us getting drunk and silly in our little town. The judge had promised to purge the file; didn't happen.

Then the list of documents for Rachel Mulligan stopped, and Rachel MacPhearson appeared.

Abruptly I pivoted the swivel chair, and stared out the window, glanced at the room's corners. Anything to avoid that name on the screen.

"All right. The whole awful truth."

A slight switch to the Bahamas provided Mac's data, including pictures of him and me at society affairs in the Bahamas. In one photo, I wore a dress we'd bought in Miami. He'd loved it, on me and not.

Next was his company's announcement about a new line of underwater robots. I was beside him the first time they worked properly; Mac had been so relieved, he'd fallen to his knees. We'd celebrated with a happy dance. Those robots would have been the precursors to Pearson.

Then a newspaper story of Mac working with the police to search for my plane after my disappearance. The photo showed him looking so worried. We were to have been married in less than a week.

In fact, I kept my wedding dress in the back of Pearson's closet.

More photos of Mac in social situations: mostly him standing alone, or with business associates. Very few of the images showed him with a smile. I used to be able to make him laugh—on command, never failed.

After that, I came across a photo of Mac and Rachel, also at a society event. Their grins were easy, happy. They stood very close to each other, touching, like they were a couple.

I had to swallow, with so much spit in my mouth.

Mac and Rachel. Undeniable.

Hunched over and rocking myself, my brain went empty. I lost track of the clock's funny beeps from the living room.

By the time Bill had begun traipsing back and forth, I stood at the window, slowly beating the glass. *Hell, let them be happy.* "They're dead now. Dead and gone, forever."

Pearson, on the other hand, had been extremely supportive—

the perfect partner. He'd gotten rid of all his sleek thirtieth-century furniture in an indestructible version of leather, after a side comment from me that I've always liked deep and cushy in some floral print. Too bad, that leather had been much more appropriate for Bill, considering his claws.

Basically, Mac had designed Pearson to take care of me—which the robot did admirably, using both traditional and unusual tools. His business acumen was a force to be reckoned with, while the study of esoteric knowledge never stopped.

Those astrology books weren't accidental. Recently, Pearson had seemed genuinely proud of me when he figured out that according to my chart I would be considered a hero someday. *Hah.*

He'd also warned me about an imminent transit of the Moon over my eighth house. When I asked what that meant, he wouldn't explain much; just said I should be careful.

A memory zipped through my mind: Mac back home, debating about Jyotish—an Eastern version of astrology—at the school of our meditation teacher, Brahmaji. Perhaps Mac had programmed Pearson to be interested in Jyotish.

Perhaps Mac had programmed Pearson to lie to me.

At one point I'd asked what happened to Mac, and all Pearson told me were the details of creating the robot that became him.

Not a hint about Mac marrying, even eventually. I could have understood the 'eventually' part, though wouldn't have wanted to know specifics.

No, it was now clear that Pearson had withheld essential information about my best friend and my fiancé dedicating themselves to each other only months after I was out of the picture.

Can. Not. Bear. This.

I began pacing. Bill traced my movements from the sofa.

Being on his first trip away from me, Pearson was scheduled

to call that evening from the furthest reaches of the solar system.

"I cannot be here," I said aloud to no one.

My dog trailed along into the bedroom, where I opened my old bag on the closet floor and began packing.

Bill sat nearby. "Where are we going?"

"I don't think we are going anywhere."

Instead of arguing, Bill jumped into the bag.

Underwear in hand, I stared. The dog could be turned off and left behind. But I didn't have it in me to do that. To save space, I left behind my collection of little stuffed animals that reminded me of home.

Nope. No longer home. Neither here. Nor there. Leaving Bill in place, I zipped the bag closed.

❑❑❑

Reporter guided to disruptive data.

Outcome as predicted by KAG84950.301.

Female human dislodged from protection of humanoid robot.

Chapter 2

After a few blocks, my high-octane emotions began to fizzle. As usual, fashionable people and tooting horns proved distracting. People gawked at my roll-on bag, which certainly appeared ancient compared with the floaters everyone else used. A teardrop-shaped taxi darted over larger vehicles, while Parisians wove around traffic and back onto sidewalks. Cold had lingered long into springtime, and thus the dank wind cutting into my self-pity, finding its way past my coat.

A flash and then a blast of thunder barely preceded the sky opening. In seconds, freezing rain poured off my head and shoulders, over my hands and the bottom of my coat and pants, also drenching my bag. The sound of my chattering teeth might as well have been a snare drum.

Everyone scattered to his or her homes. No open doors for me, though. How was I going to provide even a shack for myself, if not under Pearson's protection? Huddling under a bus shelter, it occurred to me it might be a good idea to verify how much remained from the sale of my grandfather's airplane.

Thus, some blocks later, I was dripping onto the floor of my brokerage office.

"What do you mean my money is not available?" I tried to keep my screech to a whisper—without success, judging by the heads turned my direction.

A humanoid female robot responded in irritatingly calm tones. Its skin shone the same bright yellow as the accents in the company's logo, and it sat encased in the reception desk. It never needed to go home and thus was an exceptionally valued "employee." The bot's face went blank momentarily before announcing, "An associate is on his way to assist you."

Almost immediately, a human entered the front office through a door behind the robot's desk. The guy wore a dark blue two-piece suit—or nice pajamas. A glimpse of a hive of glass-walled offices struck me as my probable fate.

Perhaps I pounced, considering how he stepped back when I spoke.

"How can it be that my capital is not available for my use?" Trying to not sound as if I doubted my own existence, I said, "A little bit was supposed to be in short-term investments." Another deep breath before continuing. "Then we divided the rest in medium-term, long-term and high-growth investments."

"You may take out the short-term money, although that account declined in value, I'm afraid. We always inform clients that no investment comes with a guarantee." He gave a tight smile. "The medium- and long-term investments recently became tied up in legal issues. And the high-growth investment..." The man reached over to use a bulky holographic screen and brought up multiple graphs and lists of numbers, on a visual that went from the ceiling to the floor. Thank goodness, it was supposedly shielded to allow viewing for only the customer. The minuscule amount blinking at about eye level was probably about as real as the images in front of me.

"The high-growth was in an almost-completed project," I said. "It should be done by now." My whiny voice was embarrassing.

He replied in an even tone that could be either comforting or maddening. "Yes, Miss. Despite being in the same zone as successful asteroids, the targeted asteroid turned out to contain not enough of the quasicrystals to turn a profit. The project is complete, as unsuccessful." He punched through several more screens, and pointed out an alarmingly small sum in green. "We could deposit this amount into an account for your use—the remainder from your short-term investment."

"I'll take this?" It came out as a squeak.

"We can have a chit ready for you in five days," he said. The guy was either brave or had no idea how to deal with a person exhibiting that much stress.

"Unacceptable." *That felt good.* "I need it soon."

The man pursed his lips, then scrolled up and down that screen, probably more to buy time than to locate information. "I believe I can arrange to have this amount, considering its size, in a chit for you tomorrow afternoon." Then he made a statement that proved he remained clueless. "Or, you could open an account with us."

Either I would destroy him, or dissolve into a puddle.

"Um, no. I will return then."

Back on the street and in a daze, I stumbled around aimlessly. Cart-bots trundled by—humanoid tops guiding their attached carts through the streets. If amidst humans, they always yielded the right of way. Robot-programing made certain of that.

All service robots were painted some vivid hue to mark them as not a person. Humans wanted to know who or what they were dealing with—a fact that forced Pearson to avoid the several planets and cultures known to hunt down and disassemble any robot approaching his sophistication.

No sophistication necessary to realize my money would hardly cover a week. "Leaving the apartment was silly." I was talking to myself, in the middle of a chic Paris neighborhood.

It wasn't a surprise that while rambling around trying to wrestle some sense into my life I'd gravitated to our street. At the corner, I debated with myself. Go back? "Yes. I should at least ask Pearson what happened." Warm fuzzies began to accumulate at the thought of talking to him.

About halfway down the block, my data pad chimed. Then again. And again.

I brought it out to check. All three messages were from the address UNKNOWN, and were emphatic:

VITAL

CRITICAL

URGENT

What if I opened a message, or three?

No words on the first, only a photograph. Of Rachel holding a baby—dressed in pink; a Rachel looking no older than I'd last seen her, and certainly not the age of nineteen when she'd given birth to her son. Baby? She had another baby?

I must be a glutton for torture, because I opened the second message.

It was a series of photos, perhaps from a gala benefit or something. A sign in one of the photos mentioned a children's hospital, and in front of the sign was Rachel holding the same baby. Then a photo with her handing the infant to Mac. Another of her walking up to the podium. Finally, her receiving a plaque.

The third message: Mac and Rachel and the baby girl, with Rachel's son Sammy standing beside them. Probably on vacation. The happy family photo-op.

At that point, rage boiled up inside me and put at risk anything within twenty feet. I turned and hailed a taxi.

The source of those messages had to be KAG8: a name that produced instant dread. For hundreds of years, that rogue computer had managed to keep its existence unknown to everyone except Pearson, all the while insinuating itself everywhere. KAG8 had haunted me these last months, following up on its threat to track my movements.

Whereas Pearson's instructions from Mac had been to assist

me when I arrived in this century, KAG8's instructions from its creator were to seize the crystal in my custody.

Before all this drama even began, my meditation teacher Brahmaji had asked me to deliver a package to Mac. Once it became clear on the planet Adalans that the golden cloth wrapped a crystal, I would have happily sold the silly thing... if not informed by someone I respected that it was a crucial Key for locating and enabling an even more powerful crystal—controller-of-the-universe kind of stuff.

Exactly why KAG8's creator wanted to control the universe remained a mystery even to Pearson.

Four months ago, KAG8 had decreed that I would set things right by locating the guru who ended up controlling the Key crystal. According to notes made by Rachel, the Master of Masters SivSatyananda had retained the little crystal, intending to use it to "avert the ultimate danger to humanity and all other life." I knew no more than that, but instinctually trusted the source.

Despite the crucial nature of that mission, KAG8 continued intent on me searching for SivSatyananda, a cosmic teacher who could disappear into thin air or pop over to another century if he wanted. That sort of stuff might seem magical, but Brahmaji would explain it all as mastery over the laws of nature because of SivSat's advanced levels of consciousness.

Levels that were so not available to me.

My gut quivered.

Despite some brave words a while ago, I was afraid. Even Paris lit up by golden sunlight through moisture-laden air, as viewed from my taxi, failed to lift my spirits.

□□□

Established: Creator of KAG84950.301, Dr. Sterling Fahlsteder, directed KAG84950.301 to confiscate crystal carried by human female upon her appearance in year 2962.

Confiscated crystal to be used to locate and seize Crystal Ceres; then to deliver message to younger Fahlsteder at his home on 3/4/1996.

Current status: Failure by KAG84950.301.

Chapter 3

The next morning, despite my best efforts and a bed like a cloud, sleep refused to remain my friend. Yawning I glanced around, trying to remember how I came to be in such an extravagant hotel room. The bed was similar to the one I shared with Pearson. The gilt furniture and brocade on every wall, however, could have been from some ancient castle belonging to one of the sixteen King Louis's.

Too quickly the "why" of the location oozed into my mind, along with a dragging heaviness—even worse than usual for these last few months. "Come on, girl," I chided myself. "You didn't lose them. They've been dead for almost a thousand years."

Still, it didn't feel that way.

Bill's first action after being unpacked was to leap around and bark. Scratching him under his chin, I asked, "You good, buddy?"

"Yes, this is a new place. Where are we?" He bowed down with his rump in the air, and we feinted one way and the other before a quick game of chase around the room. Then Bill turned and jumped up to lick me on the lips. A dry lick. Pearson had not included slobbering in the design.

Something must have caught his attention, because he plopped down and looked at me seriously while putting his paw on my knee. Bill was programmed to mimic real dogs, who use a part of their brain to read emotions. "You remain sad," he said. Soon, I had my nose nestled into my dog's neck. I knew the realities of the technology. Even so, Bill felt as real as Pearson.

Won't think about Pearson.

Like a child, soon Bill squirmed to be put down and I complied, keeping an eye on him as he sniffed around the room. He'd recently begun paying special attention to chair legs. Although incapable of adding to any smells, Bill did have a strange affinity for chewing wood when he came across it. Sometimes, Pearson had such an odd sense of humor.

With not much else to do, I settled on the bed and checked my messages. Waiting for me was a new one from Pearson, which I declined to open. I had made clear in my one communication to him that not telling me about Mac and Rachel—in effect lying to me—had been unforgivable. At issue was trust. Untruth from a human was not shocking. But Pearson, like all robots, had theoretically been incapable of giving false information. Many in my old time would have junked a computer for much less.

"Bill, has Pearson tried to get in touch with you?"

Pearson was capable of communicating with any robot, any computer, anywhere, anytime.

The Chihuahua kept his eyes on a small beetle making its way across the floor. "We interfaced. I told him you are not happy, but you are safe."

"Did you tell him where we are?"

He looked over at me. "No."

"Are you generally in contact with him?"

"He gave me to you, and my programming is for you."

"Keep our location a secret. Okay?"

"I will."

In the taxi the day before, as we drove past Parisian architecture of old stone and new twisty metal, I'd resolved to create my own life. It'd become clear that just hoping some elusive yogi would pop into my life and make everything right had become a weak excuse. Nevertheless, at that particular moment, I veered away from practical steps. Even after four months, it still all seemed like too much.

Now, alone in my elegant room, I defaulted to something quieter.

For years back home, meditation had been a part of my life, though not so much after my parents died—or at least I thought my father had died. Eventually I started the practice again, desperate for a way to deal with life. In the last few months, again I'd kind of lost it though.

About thirty minutes later, I'd settled down into the meditation; maybe even feeling good. In fact, I was feeling downright expanded.

Until two narrow cupboard doors near the bathroom popped open. Bill jumped up, barked, and demanded, "What is that?"

When I opened my eyes and recognized the contents of the cubby, I almost copied his yelp. It was a butler-bot. It took little more than a second for me to spring from the bed and hit the OFF button on the robot.

"It's okay, Bill." My heart was about beating out of my chest.

Few people, if any, would react that way to butler-bots. Cheap and efficient, they were the most common type of cleaning robot—to the point that almost every household on every settled planet had one.

The first time I came across the ugly contraptions, butler-bots gave me the creeps. A three-foot-tall collection of tubes on wheels, a half- sphere containing an "eye" capped the tallest. On top of one of the shorter tubes and on the bottom of another were mechanisms that allowed the bot to grab and manipulate items. The fourth tube was always flexible for vacuuming.

In particular, Pearson disallowed butler-bots nearby. His explanation: "A KAG8 company manufactures and services them. In reality, they are efficient data gatherers."

When I asked why he didn't tell the worlds they were being

spied upon, Pearson said he and KAG8 had tacitly come to a truce—after decades of mutually destructive and expensive struggle, hundreds of years earlier.

With the butler-bot in the closet, I blocked the door with my bag. Then picked up Bill, who had monitored the entire process, and settled back on the bed. Without even thinking I muttered, "Wonder how Pearson would explain all this with his astrology." With that my heart clinched, missing all we shared in recent months. I collapsed, face in pillow.

"My guess is that Rahu is transiting your Jupiter," replied Bill.

A peep at my dog showed him staring at me earnestly. I puffed, "You too?"

Bill using the same databases as Pearson shouldn't be a surprise, but it often was. In this case, I knew Bill was referring to Jyotish astrology, used by Pearson to explain most every situation. Sometimes that habit of his made me smile; other times I had to stifle a moan. The idea of never talking to Pearson about it again hurt.

"Pearson often replicates his database in me," said Bill. "The Parashara text is fascinating, full of rules and contraindications. Even more complicated than statistics."

"And your opinion of its validity?" The edge of sarcasm in my voice was wince-worthy.

Bill ignored the less-than-stellar emotion from his human. "I concur with Pearson that as long as an exact beginning time is known, even the life of a machine is predictable. I track your chart, also, for your safety."

With Bill in my arms I settled on the bed, hoping divine inspiration might intervene. "Whatever is happening, it's time to come up with some way to support myself." I addressed Bill, "As in, a job?" His lack of enthusiasm was probably a reflection of my own opinion.

I rubbed my forehead. "Or follow through on the information about Dad."

My father—whose disappearance off the coast of Florida right after my sixteenth birthday had been devastating. Pieces of John Alden's boat had washed ashore, but never a body.

You can imagine my shock at the cosmic surprise waiting for me on planet Adalans. Turned out, daughter had followed father through the same rabbit hole into the future.

Lately, it had become clear that I'd probably located Dad. The photo of the tall man with the same corkscrew red curls and aquamarine eyes as mine was rather conclusive. Not that I'm tall; generally, like my mother, I have to look up at people.

But I hadn't used the data to get in touch with my father.

The problem was God gas, a substance that supposedly provided a momentary "mystical experience." Most people had yet to gain any benefit, however, because the substance was exorbitantly expensive.

No one I knew used God gas—until I checked out the cyberspace site for the planet Uxmal, where my father lived.

For the umpteenth time in recent weeks I brought up the site. Audio began immediately; swelling string instruments, brass crescendo, and then a sonorous voice: "God gas. What could it mean for you?" The video went on and on about the wonderful insights people gained by using the substance and how lives had changed. No danger of addiction, the video assured.

A page or two further into the Uxmal site showed my father, get this, the king for the entire planet, with full control of God gas.

"Do you think God gas would have an effect on a dog like me?" Bill's gaze was completely serious.

I opened my mouth, and closed it again, before asking, "Do you want that type of experience?" Pearson once inquired about meditating, but then dropped the subject when I explained about the need for a human nervous system.

"My investigations indicate almost every entity aspires to more," said my dog.

Stroking Bill's ears, I said, "I don't know about the effect of God gas on you. Perhaps for a dog with a biological system the effect might be something like alcohol? You have much more going on than that, though."

What a relief he didn't argue.

❑❑❑

Prime Command for KAG84950.301: Stop Creator Fahlsteder from infecting his family with virus Zero8, on March 4, 1996, at 4:04 p.m. in kitchen of 355 South Timber Street, Toledo, Ohio, United States, North America, Earth, Sol solar system.

Instructions: KAG84950.301 must Self-Destruct, if failure at 300 standard Earth days after arrival of human female.

Time elapsed: 124 days.

Chapter 4

Shortly after that mind-blowing conversation with Bill, the com-unit beside my bed beeped. When I answered, a voice said, "Madam, you have received a package." The slight electronic twang identified the voice as the hotel's desk-bot.

"From whom?"

"The card says Captain Pearson."

I looked over at Bill, who opened one eye. "Send it up, please?" I sighed dramatically before saying, "Bill, you agreed to not tell Pearson our location."

"And I did not tell," he replied.

Rolling my head to loosen neck muscles, I faced the reality that Pearson didn't need Bill for that. On my phone bracelet, Pearson had texted twice: *Please return. All will be explained.*

"I could," I muttered at his messages. "And probably will. But I'm not ready."

After accepting the box from the cart-bot, I carried it over to the one table in the room. No tip for the robot.

The box was recognizable, at least to me. Pearson's company used a particular shade of light blue with silver and black writing. He couldn't have sent the package, however, because even he was not capable of crossing the solar system instantaneously. Perhaps someone working for him had packed it. I pictured one of the guards tiptoeing into and out of the apartment, and then handing it off for delivery. The container was so well sealed that I had to resort to using the small scissors in my toiletries bag.

Inside was the surveillance scanner. Not something to listen in on police conversations; instead, a machine to verify whether or not KAG8 was monitoring a location.

Pearson had engineered the scanner at a substantial cost.

Only after he'd brought it to the apartment had I begun to feel safe. Pearson had also been the one to operate it. Images of him checking it periodically sprang to mind. I picked up the gray metal box, surprisingly heavy for its size of six inches square by two inches high, and turned it over. Though I'd never used the device, there was no need for an operating manual. Just move the red toggle.

I flipped it. The one diode remained dark and the indicator stayed at zero.

My stomach relaxed a bit.

Maybe the contraption didn't even work. *Huh.* If not, that would be one more brick in the wall I needed to build to exclude Pearson. The monitor fit easily on the bedside table.

Despite my misgivings about Pearson, though, it was good to have an indication that KAG8 wasn't following me everywhere. If I was lucky, the computer had given up. In recent months, I certainly hadn't provided it any hope of using me to locate SivSat.

Funny how the mundane aspects of life just keep going, no matter the weirdness around you. I was hungry, and brunch at a nearby cafe seemed a good idea considering I'd eaten barely more than crackers the night before. One more expenditure in the outrageously expensive neighborhood wouldn't break my account. I hoped.

Intent on making my way down the block to the restaurant, I didn't recognize the good-looking man until he stopped in front of me, head cocked to the side and smile on his face: Turner Bishop, holovid star and general celebrity. The last time I saw him, months ago, he stood on a flight deck on the main Earth space station, unhappily watching my ship depart. KAG8 had taken over Bishop's body to follow me around that station, another terrifying intrusion by the rogue computer. KAG8 had probably abandoned Bishop on the flight deck, considering how confused the man had looked all of a sudden. The four large thugs waiting for payment probably also had been a bit of a surprise. Astonishing that Bishop beamed at me now.

"Alexa, we meet again. How fortuitous!"

"Mr. Bishop."

"Please, we are friends. You must call me Turner." He sidled next to me and took my hand to maneuver it up through his hooked arm. Although I detected no presence of KAG8, such familiarity touched off alarms. He began strolling the opposite direction of my hotel and restaurant.

I tried to steer away, to no avail. "I need to go back."

"And of course, you will. I simply want to show you something. You will be quite surprised, I promise." His hand held mine in position quite implacably.

"Where are we going?"

"A friend of mine thinks you should see something. It is unfair to keep you in the dark."

"What friend?" I asked.

"Someone you know."

The edge in those words was ominous. Human vehicles for KAG8 had struck a deal: unlimited knowledge in exchange for the risk of being touched for service. The idea gave me the heebie-jeebies. "I don't want to go."

"You will want to know this," Bishop said smoothly.

"If you don't let go of me, I'll scream."

He continued down the street, my arm firmly hooked in his. "Do you think anyone will believe your embarrassing display, after I explain about your unsteady emotional state? Or, perhaps, you would prefer traversing the short distance in the vehicle at our service?" He glanced over his shoulder. A black vehicle with darkened windows slowly followed us. "I wager you would prefer to walk. I promise we will remain on the street. It's not far. Then your trembling little self can scurry away."

Steeling myself to howl if we left the crowds, I walked along with the celebrity. People we passed grinned at him and called out his name. Women glanced at me in envy. He smiled magnanimously at them all, and allowed no one to interrupt his course.

Finally, we stood in front of a bank of news screens, tall enough to show newscasters in full human size. The screens were behind the windows on the ground floor of an office tower, and we watched from the street.

Instead of news, on the screen in front of us were three figures in the middle distance—in a park, considering all the greenery and flowers. People sat in rows watching the three. It took less than a second for me to recognize two of the people. The view changed to agonizingly clear focus, revealing tall Mac and brunette Rachel. My friend wore a long white dress. The man in the middle was saying something to them. Afterward, Mac turned and plastered himself onto Rachel. They practically had sex in front of the minister.

If I had eaten breakfast, I might be in trouble.

"Why? Why are you showing me this?"

"You have an unfortunate propensity for trusting the wrong entities." The voice did not belong to Turner Bishop. "The humanoid robot stores this clip, and others."

"Pearson would have told me about all that. At the right time. And how do you have this?"

"The robot's security is substandard."

I doubted that, but still turned my head away from the image of the beaming couple walking down the aisle, arms around each other's waists.

"Perhaps the robot would have informed you of the bare facts," he continued. "But would it have shared this?"

The screen must have been slaved to KAG8's control, because it leaped to another scene. The picture was difficult to make out, considering its low-resolution, black and white quality. Probably from a security camera. A lighted newsfeed scrolled above a dark doorway framed in old wood. Showing a date two years before I was shanghaied to this century, the feed screamed—in all caps—news of the death of a medium-grade Hollywood starlet. Her death had surprised no one then.

A memory of the doorway under the newsfeed bubbled up through my mind. It led to the back door of a bar in Nassau, in the Bahamas, that Mac and I had visited. He'd mentioned that he went to the establishment every once in a while with friends when I wasn't in town.

A woman hurried through the opening, to the toilets. The door on the left sported LADIES painted in bold letters. A minute later, as measured by the clock with a cascading stream framing the name of a popular brand of beer, a tall man walked that direction also. He remained in the corridor.

The man was Mac. I'd recognize the pace anywhere. When the woman exited through the left door, she stopped and flirtatiously tweaked his tie, and stepped into the light. Rachel. Dressed in her tightest and most low-cut shirt. I knew that stance, had seen it many times through the years: Rachel on the prowl. I'd also seen the coy manner of not resisting one iota when Mac pulled her into his arms. The same embrace he'd used with me a thousand times.

The date scrolled across the monitor again, driving home their betrayal.

Funny how a stomach can try to empty itself, even though minutes earlier it had been sending messages about being hungry.

"Soft-body reactions are unfailingly organic," sneered the non- Turner-Bishop voice.

Head down, tears blurring my vision, I searched in my pocket for anything with which to wipe my mouth. Back of my hand worked. The video continued, entwined figures moving rhythmically in the shadows against the back door.

"You received a package from the robot, the one with its own agenda." A few moments passed, enough for me to understand how completely I had been under surveillance. "Only one human can make this right. Seek that one, or bear the consequences."

Celebrity Turner Bishop spun away and abandoned me. Same as everyone else walking by who became aware of my humiliating response.

Chapter 5

After washing my mouth and showering, I sat in my room. If anything should convince me to begin creating my own life with no connections to my past, this was it.

I needed a job. Problem was, my degree from the small college near my grandfather's house in Florida had been in English. I may have learned how to think out of the box, but even at home it had been difficult to find work. Much less in the present, with robots filling all entry-level positions.

Back then, I slaved as a personal assistant for my father's cousin, an antiques dealer. I quit that job right before the fateful airplane flight that deposited me in this century, because my cousin had neglected to mention the entire scope of her plan when she offered to pay the back taxes due on my family home. Yeah, way gullible on my part. The moment of revelation remained sickeningly clear: a local sheriff at my door with a legal document stipulating that my cousin had become the new owner of my historical home. Worm. No, worms are good. Scorpion.

No reason for me to look for a personal assistant position anyway. I had so little experience with the current century that the idea of assisting in anything was laughable. I could pilot a small airplane, specifically my grandfather's Cessna. Of course, not much call for that either, even if I still owned it.

Several pages of aimless drifting in cyberspace later, the screen in front of me showed an ad for an employment agency. A few swipes here and there, and I had a page of agencies, some with offices nearby. That afternoon, I stopped at the employment bureaus and made appointments. One desk-bot even seemed optimistic when she slotted me in for a morning two days later.

Next, pick up my pitiful amount of money.

In the brokerage office, visible through the glass door, a man stood in front of the receptionist robot. People all over the office were turned his direction—some watching surreptitiously, others blatantly staring. Tall, blond, and handsome; it was none other than Iain Newcastle, son of a titled family from New Britain on the planet Varga.

More than four months ago and barely two days after I arrived in this century, Newcastle had introduced himself to me. He'd proven attentive, though mostly because his family had also wanted the crystal in my possession. I'd pretty much resisted his romantic maneuvers.

As I watched, a manager with the brokerage house stepped close to Newcastle and said, "We will, of course, contact you as soon as the next project is announced." The man took Newcastle's hand and pumped vigorously. "Sorry about how this one turned out. The asteroid business, alas, eh?"

Extremely British, Newcastle still betrayed that he was none too pleased with the gentleman.

"At least someone informed my office of this situation, because it certainly was not you. Have to say, I am disappointed in you personally as my broker. On top of that, whoever contacted me this morning wouldn't provide the full story, and thus forced me to come here to straighten it out. Make no mistake, if you had not provided the previous two winners, I would be transferring my investments elsewhere, today. "

The man appeared worried. "Did you say one of our people failed to assist you? On the phone? Do you remember a name?"

"No. And I didn't recognize the voice. Before this morning, I was about to order more investment into the project. It is unacceptable that you failed to keep me informed. In the future, only approach me with offers that are much better supported."

Newcastle didn't wait for a response. He turned and headed for the door.

Where I stood.

His face lit up.

"Miss Alexa Jane Alden." Newcastle pronounced my name with deliberate formal emphasis as he came to a stop in front of me. "What a complete surprise and deep pleasure to find you in this office. I'd heard rumors of you being in Paris."

"Lord Newcastle," I said, mimicking his tone. "'Tis a pleasure seeing you again."

"Iain, please," he said. "Or Newcastle. Third sons live a simpler life." He guided us into the corridor. "Are you here to oversee your vast investments?"

I gave a hollow laugh. "I am here to collect what little remains after a few investments gone sour, unfortunately. They should have a chit for me at the desk."

"Are you referring to an investment in a flamboyantly lacking asteroid? The one this fine firm assured us should be chock full of the stuff? Do we have something in common?"

"We might, if you also invested in that venture."

"Then we do," he said. "Where are you off to next? I'd love to take you for a celebratory meal."

Thus I could save money. "Sounds good."

❧

After collecting my chit, Iain and I began strolling along the boulevards. On our way through the crowds, we stopped at a fabulously expensive clothes shop and he asked my opinion on colors and fabrics. Iain considered some linen trousers woven in an intricate design, along with a tunic of the finest cashmere, both of a complementary gold. When I located the perfect scarf, he said, "You are a goddess." A comment that affected me beyond what would seem reasonable. But hey, why refute being a goddess?

Continuing along the streets after that, Iain chatted about weather, and Paris, and how his family was upset about his sister Penelope turning down a marriage offer from the scion of one of the highest families on the planet TohuMu.

He settled on a restaurant that usually required a reservation at least a month in advance; elegantly dressed couples waited for the off-chance table. The human maître d' recognized my companion and took us directly through the heavy drape behind him to the dining area, past the sultry diva crooning melodies. I had always enjoyed the shows at that restaurant with Pearson, but said nothing as we were led to a separate dining room.

Iain thanked the woman with, "You are a goddess."

Eww.

A human delivered our first course. As the waiter set out our plates and arranged the sauces to the side, Iain said to me, "I'm surprised to find you alone." The man closed the door behind him. "From what I know, Pearson is very careful to take care of those he protects."

I chose not to respond. If the man wanted confessions, he'd have to locate another goddess.

"How often are you in Paris?" I asked.

He smiled slowly, surmise lighting his eyes. "My family has an office in the region. Do you love the City of Light?"

I sighed. "Paris was called that in my own time, too."

"For the city to get that name, I'd always wondered whether the buildings had been lined in lights," he said. "I found out recently the name referred to the nineteenth-century Age of Enlightenment."

"Maybe it was an enlivening of the mind, but not real

enlightenment—like actually experiencing it." With that, I risked going off on a tangent he probably wasn't interested in, so I steered back. "Paris was lovely in my time, too. But it had faded from political dominance a hundred years earlier. Amazing it became a center of such importance again."

"Your references to that old time never fail to startle me," he said, shaking his head in wonder.

"I age well." With Newcastle, a certain flippancy was a good tactic. I never could tell whether he truly was attracted to me, or simply intent on a job assigned by his family.

Newcastle leaned in. "I assume you were not able to locate the man you hoped would transport you back. For your sake, I'm sorry," he said, appearing sincere. He continued in a conspiratorial tone. "Do you realize some people have heard about your adventure? It's still only part of the rumor mill, but you are becoming known." He leaned back. "And your friends, where are they? The lady, I believe you called her Rachel? And the man—I don't remember his name."

"Surprising." I carefully placed my fork beside my plate. "Donny Dixon told me your family hired him to steal the crystal from me. And that he was expected to deliver the goods."

"Well, yes," admitted Newcastle. He became fascinated with the food in front of him. "He and I may have had a couple of interactions. He never once cooperated. I would hardly have kept up with him."

I relented. "Donny was murdered by someone trying to stop us." Newcastle's look of shock was genuine.

After a few heartbeats, I continued. "You said your family kept track of Armstrong MacPhearson. Did they not also know he was married later? To Rachel Mulligan?"

"The same Rachel?" he asked, amazed. "How could that be?

She was here."

"We did locate someone connected to the man we were seeking. But because that man could take only one of us, she went instead of me."

Iain rubbed his brow. "You actually think she traveled through time."

"I know she did. Someone showed me proof that she had a full life back then."

One part of him appeared to not believe; another couldn't totally discount me. He asked, "And the crystal?"

"In a safe place, I assume."

He looked at me sideways. "Are you certain you didn't hand me the real one?" When I nodded yes, he said, "Then it must be the power of positive thinking. My family has been happy with me, delivering the goods."

Newcastle waited until after the waiter presented the second course before asking, "What about your family, back in that old time? They must have been frantic." Blessedly, he did not pursue questions about Mac and Rachel.

"My family had all died, or disappeared, before I left. I was about to create a new family. Which didn't happen." My voice broke. "Do you remember when I told you that my father was transported to this century, also?"

Newcastle considered me compassionately. "Have you located him?"

"Maybe," I lied.

He filled the rest of our time with tidbits about which companies and industries had become dominant as ocean levels rose. Over the hundreds of years since, some of the big cities had crept out of the mud, literally. They continued to struggle.

After the waiter cleared dessert and left the room, Newcastle swirled cream into his coffee. "I must know. Are you possibly," he paused, and continued in a joking tone, "running away from home?"

I lifted my head.

"Home is where the heart is," I said. "And mine is with me wherever I am."

Not unkindly, he offered, "I have an apartment."

Tempting. Staying at his place until I came up with a plan would save much money. Also dangerous, because he was watched by everyone. Heads had swiveled in his direction when we crossed the restaurant. As well, it was still possible I'd return to Pearson. No need to complicate matters.

"Thank you, but I'll be fine."

Newcastle pursed his lips and drummed on the table. "All right. But the offer stands."

□□□

Success: KAG84950.301 tricked surrogate male human into visiting investment office, thus distracting human female from humanoid robot.

Chapter 6

Sun peeking through curtains woke me the second morning. I felt better. Perhaps a job and a life would do it for me.

With the news blaring in the background while I dressed, my ears pricked at a certain name. A reporter intoned, "Chief Detective Ghengis Holmes-Fong arrived this morning to present his proposals." What he planned to solve wasn't clear. Even so, the short man whose family probably hailed from China had to be the man I met months ago. On screen, he strode across an open area with several security types trying to keep up with him. Finally, the announcer mentioned concern about an increase in piracy in the space lanes.

Holmes-Fong, with his bushy gray eyebrows, was the dear husband of Edith, a woman who had befriended me on the cruise ship from Adalans to Earth. The man had also recently returned some lost luggage to me, including an old computer with photos of Mac. Sigh. "Wonder if Edith is in Paris, too?"

Bill looked up at me. "Who is Edith?"

On the screen a virtual female began speaking. "The Galactic Council meets in Paris tomorrow, debating measures to protect the travel lanes." Photos flashed on the screen of angry people staring up at an official-type building. On the bottom scrolled the words: "Family and friends of lost crew and passengers today picketed the Council Chambers."

Besides being plain likable, Edith Holmes-Fong had proved herself more than capable. She had shared a wormhole transit with me. Actually, she did the jump and I might have supplied the extra intention to get us to our desired destination. From my conversations with Edith on the space cruiser, I knew she had a good head on her shoulders. I could use some perspective, considering I hadn't even checked out of the ridiculously expensive hotel.

If Ghengis was in Paris for a Galactic Council meeting, then he and Edith would be staying in one of only a few hotels near the Council Chambers. After I located a hotel willing to take a message for them, Edith returned my call within minutes. My relief from that tiny positive feedback was palpable. When Edith suggested we get together that morning, I cheerfully agreed. On my way there, I wondered if she would remain as friendly as she'd been on the cruise.

It was quickly clear that agonizing had been silly, considering the happiness in her trained operatic warble.

"Oh, my dear, how lovely to see you again. You cannot believe how delighted I was to hear from you." Edith Holmes-Fong, a six-foot-tall Anglo-Saxon who theatrically wore turbans and embroidered Chinese robes, had a soft embrace that comforted as much as from my aunt, many hundreds of years ago.

"Hello, Mrs. Holmes-Fong, it is such a pleasure to see you again."

"So formal! We were on a first-name basis on the ship," said the woman. "Besides, my loving husband's name could tire a tongue, if one had to enunciate it too many times."

Biscuits—or cookies—and watercress sandwiches waited at the table and Edith began pouring tea almost immediately; the aroma of black tea with a whiff of some peachy flower soothed my heart. While passing a cup, Edith asked, "How have you been doing, since we parted on the space station?"

"In India, we barely missed SivSatyananda," I said. "But his assistant transported Rachel. And a couple of days ago, a journalist showed me proof that Rachel made it back to our time." Impressive that I betrayed almost no emotion with the last sentence.

Edith, however, almost dropped the cookie she'd chosen. "Time travel. Will wonders never cease?" She leaned back in her chair. "I remember Rachel as a sweet enough young woman. Still, why give her the opportunity? You seemed intent on getting back."

I laid my head to one side. "It came down to Rachel's eight-year-old son needing her, more than anything else."

Edith reached out to briefly hold my hand, which almost undid my carefully crafted self-possession. Before I began blubbering, however, Edith asked, "So, what's going on with you these days?"

"Honestly, I'm kind of flailing. I guess I need to find a job."

"Perhaps you could work with your handsome starship captain," said Edith, coyly peering at me over the rim of her cup.

"I...I'm on my own, at least for the time being."

Edith's attention sharpened. Cup went into saucer. "Did something happen? He didn't do anything silly, did he?"

"No! No. Pearson is always a gentleman. It simply seemed time for a change. I probably overreacted."

Edith raised her eyebrows, as in, over what?

"A small lack of communication," I provided.

Edith gazed at me, probing for verification. Since Pearson always did take care of me, I didn't have to hide anything. She finally relented. "Well, all right." Edith took a sip of tea while pondering. Then she brightened. "Remember, I am a wormhole pilot."

"If it weren't for you," I said, "we all might have been killed by the pirates."

"You also helped at a crucial moment, my dear." Edith placed her teacup and saucer on the table beside her. "As a matter of fact, it struck me at the time you seemed natural in the pilot's den." She gave me a sidelong glance. "Have you considered training to be a wormhole pilot?"

It was my turn to almost drop my watercress sandwich.

"Pilot? Me?" I squeaked. "Oh, I could never do something that scientific." My nefarious cousin-slash-prior-boss had pointedly informed me more than once that I was hopeless with technology.

"Pilots for normal space are all tech wizards," said Edith. "Wormhole pilots are more about sensing our way in a space that's between space. Beyond space." Edith offered cookies, then returned the plate to the table. "There is technology involved at a certain point in a transit. Nevertheless, the more a person is fixated on high-tech, generally the less capable they are of effecting wormhole transits." She made a face. "Except, of course, those new pilots who use God gas." After a delicate sniff, she said, "With all the disappearances of cruisers, the schools and flight boards are forced to allow use of the substance, since it seems to assist. I must say, however, I have my reservations on its long-term effects." The woman gazed sidelong at me. "I suspect you would do fine as a wormhole pilot, however. What do you think?"

"It seems so involved."

"Let me know if you want to take the tests," said Edith. "I would be happy to arrange an evaluation for you. In fact, a facility recently opened in Paris because of the developing shortage."

"Mrs. Holmes-Fong?" A woman with dark eyes approached our table. Her chocolate-colored hair was intricately braided and arranged to appear a waterfall down the back of her head and over one shoulder. Her outfit skimmed over curves, and she spoke with a French accent. "I have desired to meet the famous wormhole pilot who saved the ship with many innocents aboard."

I studied her more carefully. The captain of that ship had purposely kept Edith's identity a secret, so it was curious that this woman knew that detail.

Edith looked up at the woman. "Thank you, dear. How sweet."

The woman turned to me. "And the brave Mademoiselle Alden. She also I know of."

Because I had few friends and even fewer acquaintances, I peered at the beautiful woman more carefully. Something familiar tugged at me.

The woman focused on me, and said, "Please be so kind as to pass along a message to my dearest Pearson. I look forward to meeting with him again, soon. The time together last week was too short."

"And your name?" asked Edith.

"Is not important."

As the woman sashayed toward the door, Edith moved her eyes toward me. "That was...odd. What is happening between you and Pearson?"

I didn't respond, because my mind was flooding with memories of women vying for Pearson's attention—his most intimate attention. The scene was from Earth's space station four months ago. Over the hundreds of years, Pearson had become popular with the fairer sex, for all the obvious possibilities available to a robot lover.

He had also declared for me his truest affections.

And here, slapping me in the face, were indications he had not let go of other attachments. Perhaps his programming had become far too human.

Along with all the men in the room, I watched the woman sweep through a door. "Evidently more than I realized."

All I'd need was a few days of alone time? *Might want to rethink that idea.* I glanced at Edith, who tried to avoid looking at me with pity.

Chapter 7

Half a block from my hotel, I heard an awful—and recognizable—racket: *Click-whiiiiiiiiiinnne–Click-whiiiiiiiiiinnne –Click-whiiiiiiiiiinnne*. I had to whip my head back and forth to locate the source, then rise up as tall as possible before catching sight of a certain orange cart-bot speeding away.

Normally no robot would be allowed to degrade to that point. It would either be repaired or trashed. Not this one, though. It was a KAG8 tool.

Panic barbed my skin as I fled into the hotel. No elevators waited in the lobby so I scurried up the stairs, and kept going as far as my muscles allowed. At about the fifth floor, rubbery and cramping legs made it impossible to move any further. Bent over, head pounding and heart racing, I dragged in oxygen while waiting for an elevator.

The orange cart-bot had been absent for months. Its reappearance couldn't be a good sign. In my hotel room, I bolted the door and jammed a couple of chairs against it. In the bathroom, lock turned, I paced back and forth, heart beating about four times with every step. It took forever, but finally I could remain in one place. Standing in front of the mirror, I considered my alternatives.

Edith's offer was generous, and not illogical—particularly since my options for employment were so limited. So what if I hadn't done well in any of the science courses an English major was required to take?

A message on my bracelet phone pleaded, "Can we please talk?"

Insinuations from that woman at the hotel made me crazy.

On the other hand, if I was totally honest, the fact was that

I had been using Pearson as a substitute for Mac. And I walked out on him. Who was I to cast stones?

It made sense to find out why Pearson hadn't told me about Mac and Rachel. And if I forgave him, I could return to his protection. With Pearson, I never had to think about anything. He would take care of me forever, all the way through being an old woman and to the grave. All I had to do was forgive and forget. Before I overthought the impulse, I pushed the autodial and it began to search for Pearson. The process would take minutes, since he was millions of miles away.

While waiting, unbidden memories slithered in. I tried to stop them, but it didn't work. Through the back door in my mind bloomed the image of Mac and Rachel, practically humping in the bar's dark corridor.

Mac betrayed me. And Mac programmed Pearson, thus the woman with the chocolate hair perhaps was an echo of Rachel. Therefore, the cover-up could actually have been hardwired, which meant it could arise again at any time.

White-hot anger rushed into my head. I disconnected.

By the time afternoon was disappearing into night, calm began to again find me. As I reached to turn on a light beside the bed, the scanner caught my attention. Pearson had sometimes checked the device several times a day. The box seemed to jump up at me, begging to be noticed.

Considering how easy it was to flip the switch, I did so.

Red.

It blinked red.

In a panic, I punched it off.

After a bit of time forcing myself to not search the room for some type of camera staring at me, I reached to flip the toggle again.

Blink. Blink. Blink.

The indicator pushed at 100 percent.

At that moment, being stalked by KAG8 went from theory to experiential fact. My mouth seemed full of cotton. Chest pounding, I tried my best to not give whomever was watching or listening the satisfaction of an outward reaction.

Human female informed she is monitored.

Chapter 8

If returning to Pearson was not in my future, a room in some kind of secure facility leaped to the top of my list. A call to Edith, and she immediately arranged an appointment at the Paris training center for me.

After a night in a different hotel, the next afternoon I sat at a table at the new pilot training facility. A small jiggle of nervousness raised questions about my plan. Aptitude tests were to be expected; I just couldn't conceive how they'd be structured.

"Miss Alden, have you ever taken this type of exam before?" The woman on the other side of the table paged through several screens on her tablet and carefully placed it on the table. "Edith Holmes-Fong indicated you might have some experience with space/time shifting."

"Only as in transcending thought." I watched for the glazed-over look that some people get from hearing such words, but noticed nothing. "On the other hand, I know very little about space/time and physics."

"A basic understanding of the laws of space physics before the training is important, though not crucial." The woman made a note on her pad. "That you have a concept of going beyond normal space/time may make up for the lack." She stood up and indicated a door. "Let's see how you react in the simulation pilot pod."

Ten minutes later, a technician explained that the cloth cap on my head would measure my responses. Next, he helped me climb into the egg-shaped cabinet and belted me into the chair. I began to hope the training program might actually work for me. Everything seemed as I remembered from four months ago, wedged together with Edith in the pod on the cruise ship near the star Sirius.

Edith and I had worked together to get our cruise ship unstuck from its position near Sirius, a blue giant star. Jumping directly to Earth had been particularly urgent because marauding pirates were about to tag us in a galactic game of hide-and-seek.

In prior attempts, Edith had not been able to transit the cruiser out of the system. I proposed that the crystal in my possession might assist her by tracking to its companion—the Crystal Ceres, which probably resided on Earth. Together in the pod, we each did what we were there to do, and finally transited away from Sirius, to directly above the Sun's solar plane. Maybe I had truly assisted, maybe not. There'd been no proof.

In the test pod, a soft voice over a speaker brought me back to the moment. "Imagine reaching forward in space/time," the voice crooned. "Feel the frontier, a moment or place through which to transit."

"Whatever the heck that means," I whispered to myself, and defaulted to the nearest I knew: meditation. For about a minute, all was quiet.

Suddenly, the egg spun twice and ended upside down. I hung, held into the chair by the belts. Another spin ensued, and the pod flipped over backwards twice.

This is a test, back to meditating. More quiet.

Heavy objects slammed against the pod from several directions, rocking it back and forth. The metal of the pod rang inside. Bedlam settled into more quiet, and more meditating by me.

Tremors began at the base; kind of tame at first, like a vibrating bed. But as the pulses moved up through the seat, I might as well have been in a giant wind tunnel. Higher, faster, louder, to a fury pitch.

Then silence. More meditating.

Two quick knocks on the door alerted me to it being opened. The technician's cheerful face appeared in the crack of light. "You good?" he asked.

I couldn't imagine what kind of response would be judged as correct. So, I smiled.

The technician tugged on my belts. Before shutting the door he placed two metal balls on a metal plate, on a table in front of the pod, and pointed them out. A few seconds after the door closed, the woman's voice came over the speaker. "Alexa, can you move one or both of those metal balls?"

I resisted voicing my first response—*are you kidding?*—and instead said, "Give me a couple of minutes."

The technician said, "There's a button on the right armrest. When you think you've moved the balls, push the button."

I had never had an impulse to move objects with my mind. My arsenal consisted of the one ability: to go beyond day-to-day thoughts. An experience that would result in miracles over time, though not known for moving metal balls of any size. I agreed, and closed my eyes again.

After a bit, the two little shiny balls came to mind. Which direction would they need to roll to move toward each other? Mass attracts mass; why not use the force available? How did the Russian bend those spoons with his mind? See it? Believe it? *Think it*, came to me. I watched two balls approach each other in my mind's eye. And pushed the button.

After about half a minute, the door opened and the woman smiled in a manner that gave no clue whether or not I'd been successful. I got a bathroom break and was shown the kitchen, with drinks in a refrigerator. Then back to my pilot pod. The same woman closed the pod's door and asked me to settle in and buckle the belts.

A few seconds later, she said over the speaker, "Alexa, the walls of the room will close in on your pod and will stop before touching it. Use the button again when you sense them."

The room's walls would move only under the force of a wrecking crew. So, what magic did they want from me? Were they testing the willingness of this silly wannabe?

Again I closed my eyes and settled in. The pod was totally soundproof, which of course meant that no movement in the room would be betrayed. Nevertheless, lo and behold, there, for a second, I felt—no, more sensed on some level—a mass nearby. I pushed the button.

"After the chime, we will perform the test again," came the woman's voice. "Each test lasts no more than ninety seconds." Seven times, they asked me to sense an oncoming wall. Only in two additional instances did I feel the mass as much as in the first occurrence.

Finally, the woman opened the door.

"Next, you are scheduled to meet with the director of the program down the hall." While departing, I noticed a board on wheels—like a chalkboard—standing near a wall in a dark corner. No furniture nearby restricted its movement.

The director proved to be a small man with a ring of short grey hair around a shiny bald spot. He might appear inconsequential, but lively dark eyes and concise speech betrayed a sharp intellect. He indicated that we would chat about my understanding of space/time physics.

I sat in front of his desk. "That can be summed up quickly: Not much. And what I have heard you would probably regard as quaint and old-fashioned."

It was depressingly easy to prove my assertion correct.

Afterward, I was ready for a meal and bed. Nicely, the institute provided both at a hotel next door, perhaps due to Edith's influence. Bill waited patiently in my bag.

The next morning, the first person I came across in the lobby was Edith. My heart thudded. If it was necessary to call her in, perhaps the news wasn't what I wanted to hear.

"Good morning," warbled the woman. "I insisted on being the one to tell you that you did well enough with the tests yesterday." She hooked her arm through mine and headed to the dining room. "Let's get coffee before your next meeting."

Turns out, I had correctly sensed the approaching board the three times it actually moved. No applicant had accomplished that since perhaps Edith, when she took her admission tests. One metal ball had moved. Not much, but enough to be measured by the pressure pad it sat on. And my brain waves had recovered their settled state quickly after each disturbance to the pilot pod.

Yes, my understanding of physics sat squarely at the bottom of the chart. "Even so, Mrs. Holmes-Fong assured us of a good reason for that," said the director, "and we are willing to take her word on it."

Next thing I knew, I was heading back to the hotel room to collect my belongings. The Council recently had instituted a new program of apprenticing trainees to the most experienced pilots. On a semi-military research vessel, a vacancy with Pilot Ellis Woolsey had opened. Because he had been a physics professor, he would rectify my education along with practical instructions. No, I would not execute a jump any time soon. Eventually, when Pilot Woolsey deemed me ready, I would try a few jumps by myself in a shuttle. The program was working for many students.

The scanner caught my attention, so I decided to run it again before replacing it in the bag to balance Bill's weight. Nothing had shown up the previous night.

When I flicked the toggle, the monitor showed red.

I so wish KAG8 would just disappear.

❑❑❑

Mission accomplished: Humanoid robot no longer blocking access to human female.

Chapter 9

On the flight deck in a hanger belonging to Earth's biggest space station, I followed a young woman in a white uniform with navy-blue piping. She'd met me at the entrance to the dock, after I'd trudged through several shopping areas and gotten lost in an apartment block. Surprise: people tended to personalize their front doors with screens showing favorite mountain meadows or deep space stars. You'd think details like that would help you keep oriented and in the right direction.

I was late. The woman hurried across the dock to a shuttle that would take us to the *Maria Fernanda*, a research vessel about a mile away, shining white in the constant sunlight.

"I'm Becca Hershel," the woman said over her shoulder. "It'll be nice to have another woman on board."

With those breezy words, it hit hard just how much I missed Rachel's friendship. *Rachel.*

In the short jaunt to the cruiser I almost nodded off, even considering my several hours of sleep on the way up to the space station. The effects of too much change and too little rest were catching up. The last thirty-six hours at the facility in Paris had been crammed with instructions and course basics. Gigabytes of data on my pad waited for study, or memorization if necessary.

There was a positive aspect to the quick move, though: maybe KAG8 would lose track of me. Once accepted into the training program, I'd spent the next two nights in a dorm room behind multiple secure doors. No red light on the monitor, even upon my return from breakfast.

No messages from Pearson, either.

Whacked far beyond any previous personal boundary, what I needed was a good night's snooze and a long, uninterrupted meditation or two.

The iris circled open. Air billowed in from the *Maria Fernanda*, including indications of breakfast and a kind of tang from the air cleaners. After pushing off the ceiling of the shuttle to land on my feet in the cruiser's gravity, I stepped through the disinfecting unit. I'd assumed the first brush with viruses in my new century, back on planet Adalans, would be my last. Evidently, everyone had become more careful in recent months.

After the unit made certain I wasn't introducing pathogens into the ship, it released me and I hurried past the portal officer to catch up with Becca.

I turned left, exactly in time to be almost run over by a cart-bot. As it screeched to a halt, it said "Very sorry!" before carefully wheeling around me and continuing. All types of companies depended on cart- bots. Spaceships needed the robots to cater to crew and passengers. The humanesque part of this particular cart-bot, now retreating down the corridor, was fuchsia. On spaceships, butler-bots often never left their assigned rooms.

"Your quarters are in the middle, along with the staff," said Becca.

After turning into the fourth or fifth corridor, we passed a room from which a voice barreled out.

"What the hell are you doing, Ensign?"

A portly man, dressed in the pajamas of the day and with his trousers pressed to a knife-edge in the front and back, marched out of the room, stopped in the middle of the corridor, extended his arm and pointed down the hall. "If I wanted those documents brought to me, I would have requested such. For thirty-five years, my morning reports have been left on a secured pad by my breakfast plate, in my dining room." He stepped in to pick up a pad from a table in the room behind him, thrust them at the junior officer, and waited for a response.

I angled to a spot behind my guide.

"Yes, sir," stuttered the young man. "I will load this immediately onto a secured pad and deliver it to your dining room."

"And what will you do tomorrow morning?"

"I will leave the secured pad beside your breakfast plate, sir," responded the young officer. "Which side of the plate do you prefer, sir?"

The man relaxed. "The left side, Ensign. At the ten o'clock mark. Dismissed."

After the large man shut the door behind him, my guide glanced my way and then at the floor. "You're a new apprentice in the wormhole pilot training program, yes?"

I nodded.

Becca pursed her lips. "Your room is around this corner. Don't know what you're used to. Be prepared for small—very small."

"I don't need much space."

Upon arrival, however, I probably didn't at first completely hide my shock at how little space a human might be granted. On the other hand, this sweet little closet offered very few hiding places for a KAG8 monitor. I turned to Becca. "Thanks, this will be fine. After storing my gear, unless I'm supposed to be somewhere, I'll walk around the ship. Where might the wormhole pilot room be located?"

"Where it is usually located, young woman," came a decisive enunciation from behind me, one that elicited foreboding. "Shall I prepare the two hundred and fifty souls on this vessel for a wormhole jump by an overconfident absolute novice?"

It was the man from the corridor—a male version of my scorpion cousin. "Hello, sir," I said. "No photo was offered to me? Though I bet you are Pilot Woolsey."

"You win the wager. Perhaps you desire a prize," pronounced

the gentleman. "No image of you was offered to me, therefore I took the time to request it," implying that since I hadn't, my intelligence was suspect. The man glanced at his watch. "You're late. Class began fifteen minutes ago. I expect to see you there twenty minutes ago. Down that hall, the fourth left, second right and fifth door on the right." The pilot turned and stepped in the direction he'd indicated.

Becca's face remained blank.

"Does this room have a lock?" *With which I can barricade myself safe from the galaxy?*

"Yes, ma'am." She reached around the doorway, took down a metal key and handed it over. "Good luck," she said.

"Might need it," I muttered.

Four minutes later I found the small room, where Pilot Woolsey sat at a square table. He didn't offer me a chair.

"Miss Alden, I understand you were accepted into this program because one, the Council believes in stopgap measures and loosened requirements; two, you minimally met those loosened requirements; and three, Edith Holmes-Fong recommended you."

I waited. If I'd learned anything during the tenure with my boss from hell in the twenty-first century, it was that often the best response is no response if possible.

"I also understand," the pilot continued, "that you have zero comprehension of the most basic laws of space/time physics."

Since the man stated his facts succinctly—and correctly—what could I say but, "Yes, sir."

"Just why do you aspire to the position of wormhole pilot, Miss Alden?"

Tricky. Any answer other than close to the truth, and this old codger would recognize it immediately. Tell him the whole truth and I might have to float back to the space station, holding my breath. And what exactly was the answer to the question?

I ran away from home and am too proud to return?

It's the first viable option to, hopefully, protect me from my nemesis?

It offers a method of checking in on my father?

It sounds cool?

"My life recently changed irrevocably," I said. "And from what I've seen of such pilots—including Edith Holmes-Fong—this path offers the best manner for me to create a good, new life."

Pilot Woolsey eyed me. "We will see if you are capable of walking in the shoes you aspire to fill," he said. "Historically, it has taken decades of rigorous training to bring a worthy aspirant to this moment, one that too many youngsters these days—and you, I suspect—blithely take for granted. Wormhole pilots have clawed their way up from the rank and file, rising above those who failed to tame the mind and thus bend it to the task at hand."

The pilot glared at me. "Be forewarned. Despite the Council's insistence on quickly producing more pilots, I have the ability to eject a student from the training program, with no chance of reinstatement." The man hiked up his pants. "And I have already done so, more than once."

I held on to that which I learned through hard experience in the face of my cousin: silence, if you can.

The man turned, took two steps to a table in the corner behind him, and brought back a book-size tablet. As he placed it on the table, he said, "This is a primer on space/time theory. See if you can understand any of it. You will be tested tomorrow at oh-eight-hundred."

With that, he walked out of the room.

After a deep breath, I picked up the tablet. Woe unto the liberal arts student preparing for an advanced physics test. Forget about anything so mundane as eating or sleeping. Bill would just have to wait for me in the luggage.

I took a seat at the table.

Of most importance had to be the process of transiting from one area of space to another, specifically via wormholes. Most important was dark matter, the places of its concentration and compression, and the use of human consciousness to create a bridge from one state of Newtonian matter to another. I understood that process to be similar to a person going beyond thoughts with their consciousness.

Over the hours a pattern emerged that seemed to support my assumption.

I constructed an outline of the major issues of physics, including quantum physics and the theories that developed in the hundreds of years since I took Physics 101 in college.

Sometime later, someone brought me a meal. It was Becca, who said, "So, he's got you running around in circles right away."

I rolled my head, stretching out kinky knots. "You mean Pilot Woolsey? If so, then you guessed it."

She pointed to the data pad in front of me. "Where are you at?"

"The point when they came up with an instrument sensitive enough to detect a stream of particles from an area thought to be concentrated dark matter."

"Pay attention to the dispute between the science group and the religious group. It started out logical, but has switched a few times through the years, depending on who stands to attract the most funding."

As Becca left the room, I was laughing.

Somewhere along the way, I meditated. And slept, head on folded arms.

Pilot Woolsey opened the door to the room five minutes before the assigned time. "I trust you have solved the most pressing challenges for physicists," he said as he marched in.

I didn't care whether any physicist was pressed about any challenge. I was awake only because another young officer had dropped by the room a quarter-hour earlier. Woolsey wasted no time. He took a seat at the other end of the table, and said, "You may present your version of the space/time continuum."

Two hours later, the pilot said, "Passable regurgitation. You have earned your bed for one more night. Dismissed."

Noted: Human female maneuvered into circumstance supportive of locating SivSatyananda.

Chapter 10

Three weeks of training had passed. At the moment, another concern about Pilot Woolsey's intentions bounced around in my head as the deckhands closed the hatch on my shuttle. I kept assuring myself that getting rid of me in a shuttle accident was probably not his objective.

Two evenings previously, Woolsey publicly censured me with demerits for not allowing butler-bots to clean my closet-sized space— the first time anyone had mentioned a merit system. "Tough," I'd whispered under my breath at his retreating back through the crowds in the dining room. No way was I going to allow a KAG8 minion near me. The moment Bill saw me, he demanded to know why I was angry. It took an hour to convince him that stalking the halls was not a good idea.

The previous week, Woolsey dumped the other trainee pilot onto the nearest space station. He maintained the young man was dependent on God gas. Pilot Woolsey had railed, "What if you needed to transit and you were fresh out of your little capsules? Dismissed, permanently."

When Woolsey had announced to me that morning, "You will do it now, or you won't ever," I almost fell out of my chair.

Thus, cocooned in the pilot pod of a shuttle manned only by me I contemplated a blank piece of space where supposedly a viable wormhole lurked. Even people other than the pilot insisted on its existence, so I stuffed the doubts. The *Maria Fernanda* would remain in this spot for a day, allowing scientists to study the nearby red giant star. A lack of traffic in the region made this particular wormhole a perfect testing ground for an inexperienced pilot.

Dear God in Heaven, or all around me, please help me through this, I prayed.

In the previous weeks, studying had been my full-time occupation. I now understood much more about setting an intention, certainly more than when I'd first heard the term, on the trip from Adalans to Earth months ago. The explanation then remained the best, though: an intention, or thought of a certain destination, determined the exit into space and time. Similar to the way a scientist measuring something often also modified it. The term "super strings of quantum space" had always cracked me up back in my own time, when dark matter was only a logical theory. Now, there were mercury vapor engines that traversed through concentrated areas of the dark stuff.

Exactly what I was expected to do.

I settled in the pilot pod, which was connected to and made of the same material as the ship's hull, thus making it possible for the pilot to take along the ship along through a jump, the same as his or her clothes would tag along.

Emanating from the space in front of my shuttle were weakly interacting massive particles, which was a good wormhole indicator. The hologram to my right glowed with stars and space as seen from my vantage.

I said, "Deploying Announcer." The probes, known as Announcers, activated wormholes and alerted ships on the other side that someone was coming through. Then I announced, "Engines on hold." Any shuttle's computing system documented all pilots' actions, but calling them out verbally was also the practice.

When the signal indicated no ship would be transiting from the other side, I pressed the button to maintain engines in a state that would immediately engage upon exiting.

Last step: the code for the wormhole.

In the early days of wormhole jumps, the periodic loss of

pilots was a big problem. At some point one of the test pilots mentioned that while jumping he'd heard sounds, almost a chant. Indeed, it turned out that each wormhole produced a different subtle sound. By replicating those sounds, the transiting process became more consistent and much safer. The code would begin the correct playback, which then reinforced the pilot's intention.

Becca's voice came over my headset. "Good, the engine is in the correct state." She and the assistant wormhole pilot had taken pity on me and stepped in when Pilot Woolsey insisted his time was better spent elsewhere. "Take your time, and cycle through the steps we covered. On the other side, repeat the process and we'll be here waiting for you."

"Thank you. For everything."

"Don't worry," she encouraged. "You can do this."

I breathed deep and began meditating. Becca had explained that sensing a mass approaching the ship would be the predictor of the wormhole opening up. The next step would be to "lean" myself—and my ship—into the space between. I hoped it would be similar to moving the little metal ball.

Nothing. I felt not one thing. *What if I can't do this? I have no backup plan.*

The engines started up and moved the ship away. No transit had happened.

"You're okay," said Becca. "Try again."

I did. And bless her, Becca was still there after I failed again. And again. *What if Woolsey is right?*

"How much time do we have?"

"Don't worry," she said. "Just follow the protocols."

I left the pilot pod, got a drink of water from a pouch, let out my hair and did a couple of rolls in free fall, making sure my foot didn't hit some random switch. Then I took a deep breath and again settled in the shuttle's wormhole pilot pod before sending another Announcer probe.

I meditated. Sank into silence. And finally noticed something—a mass. The "opening," however, seemed to be to the lower right, as if looking at a screw from the pointy end. I turned my attention there, and that time bliss welled up. Yay! I slid with it, on a wave, into the place beyond thought.

To a sinkhole in the mass, into which I tumbled with my consciousness.

Time ebbed and flowed, space expanded and contracted, and a subtle flow of voices like a background murmur from a crowd wafted through my mind. I'd first experienced this during wormhole transits on the cruise from Adalans to Earth—voices from the void, as if dialing from one radio station to another. I'd consistently had the same experience the previous weeks during Woolsey's wormhole jumps of the *Maria Fernanda*.

In addition, below those voices, I detected a faint sound, closer to a feeling. Maybe the chant the test pilot noticed hundreds of years ago? Before I could catch hold, though, it disappeared.

My shuttle's engine engaged and moved the craft. Engines were programed to automatically take a ship away from a wormhole, to make room for other ships coming through. Thus my shuttle moving could mean I'd again simply taken too much time in front of the wormhole. However, the hologram on my right was definitely showing a different view of space around me than previously.

I'd actually transited. Probably I looked like a startled pug dog.

Hands at my cheeks in disbelief, I checked the monitors. A ship belonging to the Maria Fernanda hovered nearby.

Daniel Wu, the assistant wormhole pilot, had been waiting for me on this side. When I apologized for taking so long to show up, he said, "Are you kidding? I've seen it take twice the number of attempts. You did fine."

With his assurances, I turned to repeat the miracle. Lo and behold, it worked again. Time moved, space opened up and closed down, and those radio voices showed up.

After settling the shuttle in the cruise ship's huge bay I walked over to Pilot Woolsey, who was speaking with the deck boss at his podium. Surely, he would be pleased that a student had made a successful jump.

Woolsey completed his conversation with the deck boss before turning. "I understand you finally transited both directions," the pilot said, "in the time usually allotted for as many as ten transits." Forget about a sliver of approval. "Your approach was off by three degrees on the first transit and even more on the second. I assume you would prefer to continue living, therefore I recommend you pay attention to that detail."

My mouth remained closed. We won't talk about what went through my head.

Then Woolsey grabbed my attention.

"You tend to dither in situations requiring immediate action. And ignore details you deem unimportant. Although you didn't quit in the face of a bit of difficulty—a surprise, I must say— you might try harder in using whatever intelligence you have to cultivate a job well done. Dismissed."

After that first wormhole jump, I took every opportunity to transit whenever the ship's schedule allowed. It got to the point that the captain of the *Maria Fernanda* hardly waited to ask the reason for my visit to the bridge. One morning, Captain Lucas simply indicated with his chin toward the first officer, who assigned time slots.

I declined, however, to mention to anyone else my experiences during transits. The voices wafting through my mind were beginning to provide bits of intelligence, despite often being only whispered words, sometimes phrases. After the first jump I had described the experience in a report to Pilot Woolsey. His response: "I am certain delusions of being a computer would be grounds for ejection from this program. Do you intend to persist along this line of idiocy?"

Frankly, I was surprised he gave me an opportunity to take it back.

Woolsey treated others the same way, but it certainly felt like he targeted me. He made a big deal after my twelfth transit, the third effort at that particular wormhole. Evidently, I went through the hole without inputting the address. Woolsey stated that was impossible. I maintained it must have happened because I'd already gone through before, so the address didn't need to be input again.

Chapter 11

Over the weeks, the heartbreak over Mac and Rachel had begun to retreat—at least, as long as that image of them in the back of the bar didn't sneak in. I wasn't ready to send a baby gift or anything, but it certainly was a relief to not have sudden rages sweeping through, or tears leaking all over the place.

On the other hand, I continued to be unwilling to reach out to Pearson. I missed him. But he'd lied to me. Okay, he'd withheld information, but it was really important information. Besides, I began to realize that I needed time away from him. Despite the constant tussle with Woolsey about wormhole piloting, it felt good to be in gear; a feeling that had steadily drained away during my time in Paris.

Regarding SivSatyananda, I never picked up a word about him in all my practice wormhole jumps. Good thing KAG8 must have decided to pester someone else. Maybe I didn't need to try to be invisible anymore.

In fact, life had settled into a nice routine.

Getting to see new planets was particularly cool. Over the centuries, TohuMu, colonized by China, had become an amazing combination of techno-maven and tradition-enforcer. Their trade fleets were a force to be reckoned with.

Planet Varga was the cerulean and emerald beauty, at least for people living in the planet's equatorial zone. Otherwise, winter white was the rule for more than half the planet's 475-day year for landmass much north or south of the tropics. When the planet had been located and settled, Brazil's space program dominated space exploration. Thus, most of the land mass had been colonized by Brazilians, to the relief of the crowded cities of Sao Paulo and Rio de Janeiro. Immigrants from only one other Earth country had been able to buy their way in. From my own time, I couldn't recall a strong relationship between Brazil and Britain, but one must have developed along the way.

Considering that the Newcastle family lived on Varga, I might justifiably feel ambivalent about visiting that planet. Nevertheless, my personal opinion didn't matter when it came to the duty roster. As of that morning above Varga, my name was at the top of the list for doing errands for the ship's scientists, despite having been tapped for service only recently. Second on the list was Daniel, the assistant wormhole pilot. His last name being Wu, maybe they'd begun taking names alternately from the front and back of the alphabet.

The shuttle we took downside was small, with hardly more room than in my grandfather's Cessna. I took the co-pilot seat, while Daniel piloted, which gave me time to do some research. Imagine my surprise when cyberspace revealed how the Newcastle family was directly related to the king of New Britain.

"Something go down the wrong pipe?" Daniel asked.

I shook my head, and maybe giggled. My grandfather had used that phrase. Daniel was on the young side for an experienced wormhole pilot, though a good fifteen years older than me and Shuttle Pilot Becca. That didn't seem to stop Becca's interest in him, however. I liked Daniel. He was always willing to help us poor aspiring wormhole pilots.

The prospect of coming across Iain or his family on Varga made me cringe. It'd be so much better if I could avoid that scenario. Considering Varga's population, it probably shouldn't have been a problem, but I didn't want to leave it up to chance.

A solution occurred to me. "Can I do the errands in Brasileira?"

Daniel glanced my way in surprise. "You mean as in, not New Britain?" When I nodded, he crushed my hopes. "I need to be the one to pick up the proof in Brasileira's capital city. I know the background, so can recognize and attest to authenticity. Besides, your travel arrangements back and forth to New Britain are already purchased. You'll stay the night there—a hotel is also arranged—and then back to Brasileira early so we don't delay the *Maria Fernanda*." I'd known about staying the night, and had turned Bill off before leaving him in my little room on board the ship. I'd just not known exactly where I'd be staying.

Supposedly, New Britain's population of almost five million had spread over an island the size of Australia. I decided to hope that statistic meant I could avoid coming across Iain or Penelope.

As we flew over the huge continent dominated by Brasileira, I piloted the shuttle because Daniel needed to repack a container. Our wash whipped the trees, which were eerily similar to the plants in the way-far-back times on Earth, almost ferny. In fact, Brasileira was situated in Varga's torrid zone, where it was the growing season all the time. Also, the Brazilian settlers had managed to build a beautiful city: full of white spires, shiny glass—and only a couple of shantytowns. Even the shuttle port was stunning. To me, shuttle ports were similar to airports, though generally sited further from where people lived.

We'd departed from the *Maria Fernanda* at five a.m. ship time. The trip to Brasileira's capital city took about four hours, where it was early afternoon locally.

"Your flight to New Britain will take about three hours," said Daniel, "but that island is to the west so you'll arrive with plenty of time to attend the royal court." He got a wistful look on his face. Maybe the culture on TohuMu was mad about royalty stuff. "The king has been holding court for a while, I understand, and Mrs. Fierro is not here only because she's been ill. Whatever the case, Mrs. Fierro is quite intent on us taking possession of replicas of New Britain's original crown jewels—for her 'research'—so you'll need to be willing to swear they are exact copies."

I tried again. "You sure you don't want to be the one to check out all that magnificent pomp and circumstance?" He deadpanned a look at me.

As with most things, Daniel was right. Three hours and two minutes later, I gazed down at the island nation of New Britain as the shuttlecraft came in for a landing. It was a good thing I'd brought a jacket, considering the island appeared to be spiraling toward winter. Either that or the trees and grass were dead. But there was a hint of the beauty available during the warmer months. The parks we flew over could have been picked up from England on Earth and dropped in place; they were so similar to those I'd seen in my old time. I recognized oak and elm trees. They must have been imported.

Walking through the airport, a voice from my recent past sent a chill, despite the extra layers. "Well. I do believe it is Miss Alexa."

Controlling my expression, I turned.

"Lady Penelope. How are you?"

"Brilliant." As in the reflection off a razor-sharp steel blade. Why Penelope continued being angry was beyond me, since Iain said his family believed they received the real Key Crystal. Penelope announced, "Pearson and I spent several days together recently. And before we parted he arranged for us to meet again. Soon." The statement had a dramatic edge, even for Penelope. She continued, "We are researching ancient codes. Among other activities."

I crossed my arms. For months, I'd wanted to work on something. Anything—and with Pearson would have been nice. That he considered her competent and capable, well, hurt. That she'd been nothing but nasty to me since the moment we'd met also definitely rankled. The next statement was out of my mouth before I thought it.

"How nice of you to spend time with him while I'm away."

"Someone needs to pay attention to Pearson, since certain others only use him."

That cut to my most private doubt. Again I spoke without thinking. "With you, does he always try to explain everything with Jyotish? When he does that with me, it's so endearing." *Bull's eye. She's never heard of it.*

Seconds passed before the blonde replied. "Of course it's common for us to consult on the subject. He shares everything with me."

A memory popped into my mind: on the space station above Adalans, Penelope had been gazing adoringly at Pearson.

Standing there in front of me, she drew herself up and said with as much hauteur as she could manage, "Whatever the case, my father is waiting. Good day."

With her struggle apparent, it finally dawned on me why she'd always been rather hostile with me. *She loves Pearson!* Guilt swept away any urge to further antagonize.

It was almost certain that Penelope had no clue of Pearson's robotic nature. Now, that didn't necessarily have to be a problem. Except for no children, any woman with the slightest desire to be protected, shielded, would be ecstatic with Pearson. On the other hand, from what I'd learned about the Newcastle family, her father would never tolerate such a liaison, because her duty was marriage and offspring.

Canterbury, New Britain's capital city, reflected those anachronistic attitudes. Almost a Tudor village, its governmental complex included a full-size replica of Big Ben and Buckingham

Palace. Horse-drawn carts wouldn't have been out of place.

About an hour later, in a teardrop-shaped taxi, I was frantically searching for the last address. The computer guiding the vehicle kept bleeping at me, "Please specify destination. Please specify destination." It started forward anyway, evidently compelled to enter the flow of traffic within a certain time period.

I was able to catch Daniel on his phone. "Hey, sorry, but I forgot which entrance I should use for the stop at Buckingham Palace."

Daniel said something about the entrance with guards wearing funny hats.

"Oh, we're right there," I said. "Taxi, stop here."

Outside the window, a backlit picture of a big crystal caught my attention. Those transmission devices had been the pride of Adalans when I was on that planet. Square clear crystals—about two feet wide, with goldish strands—had promised instant communications via any sibling device, anywhere.

"Hurry. You're late," said Daniel before he disconnected.

A quarter hour later, through an open door I watched men in crimson robes crowded together in front of an empty throne. Their funny white caps were perhaps meant as a nod to those old wigs certain British government folk used. From their excited words, it sounded like they were debating succession concerns.

While waiting for someone willing to take me through the crowd to Mrs. Fierro's replicas, I searched on my pad for information on the new transmission devices. If I remembered correctly, Iain Newcastle would have been the one to deliver them to Varga.

One sentence caught my attention: "The League of Planets made certain that all planetary governments received at least one crystal." If all planets received one of those special crystals, then communicating with Uxmal—and my father—suddenly became possible.

My mind scuttled around. When I was a teenager, it'd taken years to get over my father's death, or at least what I thought was his death. Eventually, I'd found my way through life, with the help of my grandfather and my aunt, and later my friends and then Mac. Now, with the prospect of seeing my father again, I felt an ambivalence I'd never have expected. What if Dad had become weird in the meantime? I mean, what with God gas and everything, maybe he wore tie-dyed pajamas and cultured granola into tofu patties. Okay, probably not, considering he was the king of an entire planet. But, still.

A man wearing crimson velvet and a fake feather in his cap stopped in front of me and intoned, "Follow me, please." I dropped my pad into my backpack.

The man led me through the room where the gentlemen debated. Several heads turned our way as we slowly paced near the group gathered in front of a golden throne, which blended almost seamlessly with a glittering canopy formed as a stylized version of those ferny trees I'd seen in Brasileira. All that male attention aimed my way wasn't personal, however. More, it was the herd, taking note of a lone female in the vicinity.

In front of the jewels, it took forever to verify that Mrs. Fierro's fakes, lovely as they were, were exact replicas. The originals were guarded by thick glass and an electronic surveillance system that my guide had to turn off every thirty seconds to avoid lights and sirens and possible poison gas—so he maintained.

On the way back to the entrance, I retraced the path near the male confab. One beaming fellow was receiving hearty backslaps from the other be-capped gentlemen when we entered the room. Everyone's attention was on him. He, however, began watching every step of mine through that room. I almost stumbled when I first noticed him, but was able to keep going. No, it wasn't Iain. But similar, and beefier. Somewhat disturbing: upon sight of me, his prior glee had changed to almost a scowl. *What? Had Penelope griped to him, too?*

Eventually, I stood on the palace steps. It was from there that I noticed the Royal Communications Building. Even from a block away, another glowing screen could be made out, publicizing the beautiful two-foot-square crystals, clear with golden threads.

Struggling with the rather bulky bag, I blundered through that building's entrance. A man had been about to exit, but he stepped aside to allow me through. I froze mid-stride in the doorway. This guy also had to be related to Iain, though less brawny than the man in the throne room. His fair hair just touched the collar above broad shoulders. It appeared he thought I might be unhinged, considering the way I continued to block the exit, but he didn't seem to recognize me at all. I managed to start moving again and we both went our way.

Inside the office, a quick peek around the room showed no one else I could identify as part of the Newcastle clan. *Yay.* A real human woman stood behind the desk. She responded to my question about calling another planet with the words, "Fill out this form." Only at the bottom did I notice the cost: five minutes speaking time would take more than two weeks of my wages. I gulped.

"We are closing early this afternoon," the woman said. "I suggest you put in your request and we can schedule you soonest."

"Tomorrow morning?"

"We open at eight a.m.," she said, sounding doubtful.

On the edge, I said, "That's fine, though I'd have to leave very soon after eight." The woman looked at me as if I was crazy. I said, almost in a little girl voice, "This will be a call to my father, who I haven't seen in almost twelve years. Please, can we try?"

The woman relented. "If you arrive here in time, we can try. I cannot guarantee, though."

I signed up for the first slot the next morning.

At the hotel, the rest of my time was free. I savored a long meditation, then a tasty dinner in my room while watching a docudrama I'd gotten hooked on. After a quick shower, I used one of the scented lotions that worked wonders on dry skin.

Happily, despite all unanswered questions of the day, I could hardly keep my eyes open. Regarding the call to Uxmal the next morning, I decided it didn't have to happen. I could simply not show up. A sound like an air-conditioner turned on, lulling me to sleep. Right before I lost consciousness, my muzzy attention noticed a prick on my arm. *Must be a sharp edge on the bed somewhere...*

Strange dreams that night—whispers, lights—perhaps due to the spicy food. Didn't matter though, since I easily woke up in time to arrive the next morning at the Royal Communications Building, ten minutes before the office opened.

□□□

Human female extracted from ship.

Chip embedded.

□□□

Being the first one in the Communications office had its benefits.

The woman put me through immediately, before I could chicken out. On the other end of the line, a lady announced, "Uxmal Telecommunications. How may I help you?"

"Hello?" At that moment, it struck how silly it was to simply call and ask to speak to the king of the entire planet. "I...I'm calling for John Alden. Is he available?" No video; evidently they saved that for the real conversation.

There was silence on the end of the line. A male voice came on. "Who do you want to speak with?"

"May I speak with John Alden, please?"

"That will not be possible."

"Please, I have very little time. Would you tell him Alexa Jane is calling?"

"This is highly unusual."

"If you tell him the name, I think he will want to speak to me. I beg of you."

"I cannot believe he would arrive quickly."

Reluctant to say much more, I turned to the operator. "Can I hang up now and call back, with the leftover time?" On a nod yes, I turned back to the receiver and said, "I will call back in five minutes. I promise you, he will want to speak to me. We are calling from," I checked the code, "New Britain on Varga, Code 5336. Please, at least try."

"I will. But it is unlikely he will be here."

I walked out of the booth and took a seat. Time was short. I'd paid my money. And now that I'd actually taken the first step, I hoped beyond hope it would happen. Hearing people even close to my father brought all those vague wishes into clear focus.

The office was filling up. The blond man from the day before strode into the room and walked behind the desk. Considering how the women spoke to him, he probably had some type of official position there.

Three minutes later, the lady who had been helping me called out, "Miss Alden?" She looked up from behind the screen where she worked and called my name again. When I waved at her, the woman checked her screen and said, "You have an incoming call. Enter booth number five."

I ducked into the booth as quickly as I could. When I picked up the receiver, an imperious voice boomed, "Who is this? What do you think you're doing?"

My father! My heart flipped, jumped up and down, did a wave from one side of my chest to the other and back again.

"Dad? It's me, Alexa." As I was finishing my words, the image of my father appeared, tense and angry as he spoke, the image lagging the words by a few seconds.

"How dare you try a trick like this? Whoever you are, I will hunt you down..." He stopped short. My image must have made it through to him. His image bent close to the screen. He shook his head.

"Dad? It really is me. Really. Truly. I promise." I wiped a tear from my cheek.

"Alexa?" His face crumpled and his bottom lip quivered. His mouth voiced my name.

"I got sucked into the light thingy, too, Dad. Murdoch Callaghan on Adalans didn't know where you went." He looked concerned. "So I took a job that might help me find you."

With a smile at him, I shrugged.

"And there you are, in front of me, impossible as it may seem." His mouth opened to speak. "Where are you? I must see you, hold you. Make sure you're really here."

The beeping light indicated fifteen seconds.

"I'm on my way to you. Maybe in three months. Are you really king of Uxmal? Anyway, I love you. I'll send a message." As the image of him listening intently to me faded, I touched the screen. It would be so easy to pay the rest of that month's salary for more time.

Leaving the booth, the lady said to the blond man, "George,

would you mind approving this?" I waved to her on my way to the door. While she was waving back, George maneuvered to look at the screen in front of them; then over at me, surprise on his face.

❑❑❑

Parent of human female detected.

Point of vulnerability.

Chapter 12

A few weeks later, before leaving for the *Maria Fernanda's* flight deck, I put Bill to sleep and scanned my room for a KAG8 monitoring device, despite the fact that computer continued to be absent from my life. True, a tiny spike showed on the monitor. But no light. Sometimes electronics do wacky things. I promised myself to try to find someone who could verify the thing worked correctly.

The night before, I'd snuck over to the other side of the ship to check the hiding place for a certain package sent by my father. The fruit he'd sent was rotten by the time it arrived and the flowering plant had been frozen somewhere along the trip. The catlike figurine was gorgeous, however, and very much worth keeping. The contents of that figurine I'd hid in an air duct far from my room. Except for one capsule. In his note, my father requested that I always keep with me some of the God gas, explaining that the substance had become currency in some places. "I want you to always be able to take care of any emergency for yourself."

In fact, taking care was very much on my mind that morning, because I was on my way to what had been decreed to be my final test.

Pilot Woolsey continued to appear offended that I remained in the program. After I passed the extended physics exam, he said, "I have no more time to waste. If you complete this next wormhole transit with not one problem, I am rid of you." Then he raised an eyebrow. "On the other hand, if you require assistance in any manner, you are out of the program. Is that clear?"

Yeah, as clear as a fantasy of my fist connecting with his chin.

Several science teams checking out an asteroid belt were using the best shuttles. No problem, though, since the one shuttle available was the type I'd done my training on. I made certain to drift away from the cruiser to a safe distance before powering up the engine to travel the more than seventy thousand kilometers to my destination.

In position at the wormhole, the shuttle's green indicators glowed appropriately and the reds were safely in their zones. The weakly interacting massive particles in the area scanned a bit different than usual, with lower gravitino and gamma ray levels than noted in the pilot's database. But because the database didn't say it should be a problem, I simply noted it for later questions. With eyes closed, I settled in and began meditating before the transit.

Wormhole transits affected people in some funny ways. Many lost consciousness, even if in the middle of a conversation. In fact, cruise lines tended to schedule jumps during night shifts for that reason. In that first cruise, I'd reacted similarly, but now I mostly just felt a tug toward unboundedness. Not a bad thing.

In the shuttle, I felt the mass of dark matter move toward me, closer, closer. There. My consciousness and the mass kissed and I leaned into it. The flow of voices appeared, as usual, even continuing the trend of separating, cresting in waves, into potentially viable information.

On the other side of the hole, sensors around me were all within normal ranges. I could have simply opted to start the engines and travel back toward the event horizon, but I loved taking in the visuals of a new space.

When I checked outside the tiny window, rainbows of light rippled around the shuttle—Earth's aurora borealis on mega doses of super- vitamins. In the distance was a pinpoint of intense light, probably the star for this system. The database said the star was on its way to becoming a white dwarf.

A rocky planetoid hung nearby. That told me something was wrong. Wormholes tended to be found away from the disk of planets in a system.

Sensors verified the planetoid and several additional nearby bodies to be in orbit around a gaseous planet. Since I only saw deep space through the flickering colors, the planet must be directly behind me. Supposedly, that planet had the mass of more than fifty Jupiters. A fact that would make it much closer to being capable of igniting—and thus creating a binary star system.

I pulled back, stunned. It appeared the wormhole had exited me near a gas planet. Did Pilot Woolsey send me into a potential gravity sinkhole on purpose? If so, I had cooperated by not reading the database back hundreds of years to when this system was first found. Point for him.

The lights might be fascinating, but I needed to move away from the combustible gases around my ship. If I ignited the engines, could the vessel be turned into a flash point? And what about the bigger question: could I even break free of the gravitational pull of the giant planet right behind me?

"If I do," I muttered, "I'll bring proof of everything."

Turned out that my shuttle wasn't actually within the gas planet; rather above its thermosphere. Close to the dividing line between the lower part of the atmospheric layer—where the aurora borealis displayed its colors on Earth—and the upper part of the layer. That's where the space station would be situated, if this were Earth. It would have been nice to have the safety of a space station nearby.

Engrossed in documenting my situation, I barely glimpsed the tongue of green and blue light before it licked my shuttle, up and over into a roll. Deep space in the window was replaced by a mottled orangish brown color. Then space, and then again the orangish brown.

Struggling to avoid hitting a crucial switch or button as I bumped off every imaginable surface, some rational part of me identified the out-of-control tumbling as the immediate danger. Colors quickly losing their intensity could have been a good sign, since the combustible gases were perhaps dissipating. I didn't have time to wait for verification though.

Safe to use a thruster? My internal voice, the one I could depend on to tell me the truth, said yes. I prayed please and tried for a tiny burn.

The first burn didn't help. But at least nothing outside the ship ignited.

The second one slowed the roll a bit.

The third reacted in the wrong direction. Panic prickled. More small bursts, and slowly the rotation stopped. It seemed like hours, though later the chronometer showed only twelve minutes had passed.

When I finally had a chance to check my position, indications were that the ship had rolled away from the planet. If I'd been in a gravity environment, I would have done a happy dance.

"Okay, first, let's find the wormhole." From the database, it should be right "there," I whispered. No traces showed of the subatomic particles that normally spewed from wormholes. I checked again. Still nothing.

The database mentioned nothing about this hole exhibiting this type of behavior. On the other hand, I noticed the trick Pilot Woolsey probably hoped to catch me on. Considering the wormhole's usual position above the mass of the main star and this giant planet, hard experience had proven a pilot had to approach the wormhole exactly head-on, not even a partial degree off. If I got out of this, I resolved to read every word of the pilot database.

The immediate issue remained the challenge of locating the wormhole's event horizon. How to approach it head-on, if I didn't know its location?

An hour later and floating over the shuttle's control panel, I checked my plan for about the fifth time. Then an Announcer from the other side lit up the wormhole. Pilot Woolsey was about to transit through to claim his victory by rescuing me.

But no shuttle exited the wormhole. *Whew.*

At least its location was clear. The wormhole had, indeed, drifted from its standard position and toward the gas planet. I fired the shuttle thrusters in microbursts. When an Announcer lit up the wormhole again, I waited; still no shuttle exited. But the hole was definitely moving.

Taking care to approach the wormhole exactly head-on, I advanced, closer, closer. Again, an Announcer lit up the location, and no shuttle exited. The wormhole had shifted an entire degree.

After modifying to allow for the implied path, I meditated, felt the mass, and leaned in.

The mass pulled away.

Maybe I'd taken too long.

I moved the shuttle into place again, closed my eyes, did everything correctly. Afterward still the gas planet loomed. No transit.

Drag from the huge planet? *If so, how will I ever get out of here?*

I had a God gas capsule, which according to Woolsey's rules could be considered cheating. Staying in that situation would be unacceptable, however.

Grimacing as I extracted the capsule from a double-zipped

pocket, I held it in my fingers in front of my face. With the dashboard lights making a halo around it, a stray thought about my father as a God gas pusher zipped through my mind. "Hey dude, take advantage of a sale on exalted states of consciousness—today only." Chortling, I wondered if the effect could happen from just holding the stuff.

The golden-brown grains filled the capsule only halfway. What did Uxmal's site say? Breathe it? Swallow it?

"Breathe it," I whispered and broke the capsule. It smelled like sandalwood. After a delicate snoot into each nostril—and barely managing to not sneeze the stuff all over the walls—some of the substance remained in the capsule so I carefully recapped it and put it back into my pocket.

No immediate impulse to roll around in hilarious guffaws overtook me, so I waited.

After sixty seconds by the dashboard clock—it took forever—I resisted the urge to inhale the whole thing. Instead, I began meditating. Ah, there's the difference: no thoughts. Usually while meditating thoughts were a given for me.

This time, a sense of expansion immediately began to spread, like the sun dissolving a cold morning's frost. First, I felt like I was out of the ship; then I expanded, past the planet; out of the solar system; then through the boundaries of the galaxy, to beyond. I was in my body, but also part of All There Is.

Sweet.

I could have happily drifted like that for eternity, but reminded myself the goal was to get out of this solar system. I inched the shuttle toward the wormhole. Then closed my eyes again. The mass was near. I leaned toward it, eager.

Nada. Stranded in the midst of nothingness.

Indeed, the hole had again drifted away from my exact head-on course. So I corrected the shuttle's entry and tried again. This time, a few seconds passed and the voices showed up in my consciousness. *At last!* Even a visual, kind of. Bits tracing through the wormhole, like data through the Internet, a brand new experience for me.

But I was so happy for the transit to be happening that I ignored it. Some part of me almost cried in relief.

Then something else flowed in my awareness—subtle, the echo of a smell. Unpleasant. Reminiscent of the feeling of KAG8 in the forms of Corky, and Varshana, and Turner Bishop. The impression disappeared when a familiar energy surged through my chest.

The *Maria Fernanda* waited for me nearby, glowing white and safe in the light of the nearby star.

On board the cruiser, Captain Lucas ordered, "Take her to medical," as they guided my float pallet away from the shuttle at the dock.

Looking on was Woolsey, who turned and strode away while muttering something about God gas.

□□□

Potential demise of human female discerned.

Fact: Activating Announcers deemed hazardous to anonymity of KAG84950.301.

If human female is lost, no known equivalent path to SivSatyananda.

Resolved: Increase motivation of human female to locate SivSatyananda.

Chapter 13

A few weeks previously, an advertisement for one of Pearson's companies, the one that tracked robot parts for safety and recalls, scrolled by on my pad. For a bit I'd felt strange, considering how I was no longer part of his group. No further messages from Pearson had ever shown up, but I was okay with that because I remained unwilling to communicate with him.

KAG8 must have lost track of me, considering the total lack of creepy visitations in the almost four months since leaving Paris. Good thing, because in spite of the implied threats if I didn't locate the wise man SivSatyananda—and thus the Key Crystal—not once had I come across even a mention of that man.

Someone else who might have forgotten about me: Woolsey. In the more than two weeks since the drifting wormhole fiasco, Woolsey had yet to approve me out of the training program. I chalked it up to the two new apprentices he had to persecute.

Early one morning shift, word came down that some of the crew would visit a new outpost on a marginal world. The planet had one type of weather—sweat-streaming-off-your-body summer. The colonization plan had been that if the suckers, er, settlers cleared enough forest, the group might make a go of it by providing fresh food to the two space stations within a few days' travel time. Captain Lucas was a fan of ripe fruit.

Daniel transited our small freighter into the system. During the jump, I picked up on the normal stream of voices. Usually, that experience was mundane, even cheery. This time, there was a darkness, an anger. The blue and white planet in front of us was so beautiful and similar to Earth, however, I happily let go of the idea I should trace the source of the anger.

Becca piloted the ship. To leave more storage, the freighter's bridge was small. In the twelve-by-eight foot space, Becca sat about halfway back from the front, where the pilot pod was always located.

As Daniel moved around in the area, checking readouts on the walls and the massive command station between the captain's chair and the pilot pod, Becca prodded him to hurry up. Funny how despite the years between them, they bickered like an old couple. When he exited the pilot pod a third time, she said "Could you please clear the buffer when you're done?" I got the impression she'd brought this up to him a million times. Dan didn't respond. The other two scientists ignored the interaction.

It was a relatively short and simple trip from wormhole to planet. Becca turned to me after putting the craft on autopilot. "Are you aware of what went on between Captain Lucas and Woolsey?"

"When?" I asked.

"While you were on the other side of the drifting wormhole," she said. "I heard the captain was on the verge of spacing Woolsey." I looked at her as if she was missing a few atomic particles. "No, really," she protested. "On his way to the bridge that day, Woolsey was whistling. I heard it. But when he showed up at the bridge, the captain nailed him." She mimicked the captain amazingly well. "'Mr. Woolsey, please explain to me why you sent a pilot-in-training through a wormhole emitting these signatures.' A friend of mine put the data on a screen. Everyone saw it. Ammonia, nitrogen, methane, carbon dioxide. Only science mission shuttles can detect those things, and you weren't in a science shuttle."

"Might have helped if I had been."

"Woolsey asked if they were certain the emissions were from

94

the wormhole. The captain actually got red in the face. That's when my friend wondered if they would have to look for Woolsey somewhere out an airlock."

Daniel floated past the two scientists belted into the seats in the back part of the bridge, approaching Becca and me. "In his defense, Alexa," he said, "that wormhole was the perfect test. Because of your tendency to slide over standards."

Becca broke in. "All hell broke loose when the Announcer tubes began firing themselves."

"The deckhand said something about a mystery firing of them." I wasn't about to disclose that the Announcers had made it possible for me to return to the *Maria Fernanda*.

Turning to work the com-panel, Becca glanced my way and said, "Nobody can figure out how it happened." She glanced over at Daniel. "Not even Woolsey."

Above the planet, there was no response to our inquiries. Becca tried several more times. "Dan, do you pick up anything on your instruments?"

"Check the 4040 kilohertz band, you always forget that," responded Daniel.

She flipped switches, punched buttons, and paged several screens of data. "Says here the transmission equipment down there is brand new. And no record of frequent power outages."

We were debating on whether to land anyway when over the speaker came the words no one would want to hear.

"Prepare to be boarded."

The voice could easily have also uttered 'resistance is futile.' On screen and too big for comfort was the visual of a fighter craft that looked capable of taking us out.

"Punch it," yelled Daniel, as he wrenched open the pilot pod door.

"Duh," muttered Becca, though she didn't hesitate to jink this way and that to avoid the fighter ship's early warning shots, while also pushing our ship to its limits toward the wormhole.

The odds were not good, considering how the fighter began pouring on the lasers and we had nothing to fight back with. Agonizing minutes dragged by. We all monitored the life-support indicators.

The distance between the wormhole and us was small, I could sense it.

Daniel yelled, "A little closer," before slamming the pilot pod door closed.

Glancing blows sent sparks off the instruments.

But Becca was good, or our attackers were inept. When we drew near enough to the wormhole, Daniel fired the Announcer. Becca didn't even pause for a response.

The fighter craft moved to our side. Becca jerked our ship up and down to avoid their laser fire. Make that mostly avoid— the effect of glancing strikes from that ship burned holes in my clothes; also for the other scientists, judging by the squeals.

"Dammit," muttered Becca.

I tried to keep out of her way. The two scientists mostly kept their terror to themselves, yelping only every once in a while.

Daniel almost had us into the wormhole.

Then we took a hit, right on the pilot pod, which flared out in flames. No way to avoid the reek of hot metal, crisped electric wires, and other smells.

"Dan!" Becca's scream was tortured.

One of the women unhooked her belts and grabbed the fire extinguisher; her partner whimpered, but did the same before moving toward Becca, who seemed to have forgotten she was piloting a ship. The scientist and I frantically brushed burning pieces of the ship off of Becca and our clothes.

Finally, Becca tore her eyes off the smoking pilot pod, and swerved our ship toward the fighter. For a moment, I was afraid she might be suicidal. The scientist and I glanced at each other in shock.

Then the fighter backed off in an avoidance maneuver. Becca knew what she was doing, and we were in one piece, not spewed into the vacuum of space.

The wormhole was still open. I felt it.

"Keep going," I yelled, while launching at the bulkhead. I aimed at the only bare spot on the wall.

Becca cried out, "What can you do?"

If I touched the metal connected to the outside of the ship, maybe I could make the transit happen.

"Just keep going!" Worst case—very worst case—we'd zip through empty space and be taken over by the pirates.

Holding my body against the wall, which remained blistering hot because of its proximity to the wrecked pilot pod, I prayed the wormhole address. When all the right things for a transit began to happen, I almost whimpered in relief.

Before we got through, however, over the speakers sounded a voice I knew too well.

"You were saved by the Announcers for a reason."

Space opened, and the radio sounds flowed in my consciousness.

⌒⤬

On board the *Maria Fernanda* a week later, I was barely ready to be around anyone other than my dog.

Except for Becca. In fact, I'd spent a lot of time with her. "Becca, please eat. You like this." Slumped, wedged into the far corner of the bed, legs drawn up to her chest, she never said a word, except for berating herself. Then I'd locate another handkerchief for her.

Daniel's memorial had been quietly attended by the entire staff, and many paused to speak to Becca. Even Woolsey, who for the first time seemed to be at a loss for words.

While Woolsey fumbled condolences, the scientist who'd helped me with brushing off the sparks—Rodri was her name, I think—leaned over and whispered to me, "Did you hear someone say 'saved by Announcers' right before we got through? What could that be all about?"

I glanced Woolsey's way, and just shook my head.

The thought that KAG8 had actually saved me was deeply unsettling. *Just how much has that computer been watching me?*

Early the following week, the captain offered a new training session on weapons use. Yeah, a little knowledge might be dangerous, but the more pressing problem was not enough people able to work the space cannons. One of the few times Becca left her room was for that training. I went with her. At the session, Becca muttered, "For Daniel," as she slammed her fist on a non-working laser button.

A few days after that, we arrived at the biggest space station I'd ever seen. We were there to pick up new scientists, but everyone was looking forward to some down time.

That station was more coherent than most, because the designers seemed intent on building the sphere outward, instead of the usual glomming-on of units connected by tubes. Expansion had been going on for five hundred years, someone told me. In fact, if a rocky core could have been engineered the station might have attained the status of planet. It was called Diego Garcia, due to being in the middle of nowhere.

The morning of arrival, everyone was rushing around to ready the ship for the new scientists, and I was a little late for breakfast.

Pilot Woolsey came to a halt in front of me near the ship's mess hall. As usual, he refused to address me by name.

"The accreditation board in all its flaming brilliance granted a second-class commission to you." His face betrayed both distaste and iron control. It seemed like he might say something more, but instead shut his mouth so hard I heard the teeth come together. He spun around and marched away.

After a moment, my mouth slightly agape, I stepped out of the way of traffic. After the food line, tray in hand, I noticed Becca at a table and asked to join her. It was good to see her someplace other than in the corner of her room.

"Of course," she said, and indicated the chair across from her. "Congratulations on your commission."

"I was beginning to think they might toss me from the program." As I picked up my fork, I asked, "What does second-class commission mean?"

Becca responded with, "Dan said..." Then she stopped. Her eyes teared up, but she didn't cry. After a deep breath, she continued. "A second-class commission is what they do in this new training program. It means you are still training under whoever is the number-one pilot. I believe it's a conditional approval to be reviewed in six months." In a quiet voice, she said, "You know, if you took the assistant position on the Maria Fernanda, you'd stay around. I'd like that."

Remaining in the vicinity of Ellis Woolsey would be my never-choice.

"Hanging out with you would be awesome. But can you see it working with Woolsey?"

The look on her face gave me my answer.

Captain Lucas and I passed in the corridor on the way back to my room from the mess hall. As usual, he wore a uniform as white as his hair, crisp cotton tight across his shoulders. The captain asked me to follow him to his ready room, where he formally congratulated me. He never played favorites, but I got the sense that he enjoyed training new staff—the opposite of Woolsey.

The way Captain Lucas sent off a message to the duty officer that I should have station-leave for the next several days gave the impression he might be thinking along the same lines as me for my future.

On the Diego Garcia space station, the wall screens with their constant stream of news caught me up on everything going on among the various settled worlds, as well as celebrity gossip. Really, no different from a thousand years earlier.

As I was about to turn away, another screen caught my attention, one with that intrepid newsman Zaire Chevalier— bearer of those life-changing revelations about Mac and Rachel back in Paris. Zaire must have gotten a new beat; I didn't remember him covering astronomy.

"News today about a mysterious space shockwave coming our way," he said, dreadlocks primly clipped back and twirled into a single braid.

A graphic came on screen of our galaxy as theoretically viewed from above. I'd never realized how close the human-settled planets were to each other, relative to the rest of the galaxy.

A visual was added to the graphic, like the wave in front of a boat. A recently settled planet named Zubhra would be the first humanity affected by the bow shock, then the Diego Garcia station.

Barely a year ago for me, back in my old time, it had been big news when the Voyager space probes made it into deep space, by breaking through the Sun's bow shock.

Zaire continued. "Astronomers conjecture that an event more than ninety thousand years ago in the center of our galaxy may have ejected whatever is behind this shockwave—one that's on a collision course with the human nexus of planets. A multi-discipline team of scientists is trying to analyze the crucial light-wave spectrums to identify what's creating that shock wave, but dense space dust is complicating matters."

Zaire's story was then interrupted by a newscaster droning about a takeover battle between two companies.

So, I turned to the three-dimensional maps of the station. Most stations provided sections for particular professions, including one for wormhole pilots. I'd always been too shy to visit the wormhole section before. According to the map, the wormhole pilot region on this station was smaller than for regular space pilots or for metal workers or engineers. Nevertheless, it now officially offered a haven for me.

I strolled a long ramp amidst crowds dutifully walking on separate sides—me on the right and those headed the opposite direction on my left. Chatter filled the air from parents with small children, groups of teens, and from workers who had been cleaning a big mess judging by their grunge from head to toe. Then I headed down two steep escalators. Elevators were somewhere nearby, both those similar to what I was used to in my old time for freight and a kind of free-fall-type tube, but I liked watching people.

Past the section for regular pilots was an entry for a cerulean corridor, and on the wall glittered a four-foot version of the logo on the shoulder pins presented to me by the *Maria Fernanda's* captain—a yin and yang symbol with a cerulean background. Further along the concourse were bars and restaurants, and a hotel at the other end. The most official-looking façade housed the Wormhole Pilot's Association.

Inside that office, an older woman sat behind the front desk. Four people studied a screen on the wall to the right. The door behind the woman opened and an older man exited, smiling hello to the lady at the desk before strolling over to the foursome.

"Hello there, are you new pilots?" he asked the three young men and one middle-aged woman. They nodded in his direction. The man continued, "Have you signed in with the association yet?"

The woman at the desk chimed in. "Yes, Cyrus, they signed in and verified themselves. They're checking the postings board now." A mention of postings perked me right up. At that point, the man glimpsed me.

While allowing the door to close, I said, "Hello. Perhaps I should sign in, too? I recently received my commission."

"Excellent," he said, looking at me. "Come over to my desk."

Pilot Cyrus Ulysses had worked me about three-quarters of the way through the process before he paged through to the next screen, stopped, squinted his eyes, scrunched his eyebrows together, and looked over at me.

"You completed an apprenticeship with Pilot Ellis Woolsey," he stated, with no inflection. "You were also the one to get the shuttle through the wormhole before the pirates were able to capture it?"

"Yes, sir." I wondered what caught his attention.

"Are you aware Pilot Woolsey filed a protest over your commission?"

Somehow that didn't surprise me.

Pilot Ulysses paged through a couple of screens. "It seems the captain of the *Maria Fernanda* recommended you for this commission, with high marks." He continued reading down the page. "And your commission was approved, despite Pilot Woolsey." The man scratched his neck for a moment, then tugged on his earlobe. "Would you be interested in a bit of advice from a wily old codger?"

With a smile from me, he said, "Find a berth to keep you out of sight. If I could do my piloting career over again, I'd avoid hoopla involving my name." With a glance past me toward the screen and the people in front of it, he said, "Afraid any vessel there wouldn't fit the need. And besides, there's a glut of second-class commissions. How creative are you?"

Dilemma for KAG84950.301 remains: Self-destruct command if failure at 300 days after appearance of human female in year 2962.

Status: Failure continues at 243 days.

Resolved: Incentivize human female.

Chapter 14

A search of databases showed plenty of ads from hopeful wormhole candidates searching for a position, but almost all of the pilot ads stipulated no second-class commissions. Very quickly, it became clear the *Maria Fernanda* was no longer the place for me. Anywhere near Woolsey was more frigid than deep space.

While searching the pilot want ads for the third time that day, a message popped in from my father. "Dearest, didn't you say your ship would be approaching Uxmal sometime soon? I have a grand reception waiting for you."

Visiting him now would at least get me away from Woolsey. I tried to convince myself that after some time passed, demand for second-class wormhole pilots might pick up.

Once committed to visiting my father, I worked out a scheme to put KAG8 off the scent by signing up for a trip on a vessel going the opposite direction from Uxmal, trips via spare berths being a benefit available to pilots. I even checked in and took control of the room. On the *Maria Fernanda*, Becca sent a message to my father about my real plans.

I said goodbye, covered my hair with a hat, and made my way through the space-station crowds to the ship that would take me to the man I hadn't seen in more than a decade. Each night of the three-day trip, sleep eluded me. Each day, I watched families and how they interacted, and tried to talk myself out of building up expectations.

On the ground on planet Uxmal, the spaceport was crowded with what looked like a thousand people milling around on the tarmac.

Through the shuttle's open door, slightly Latin tunes from painfully new synthesizers, antique brass trumpets, and a few conch shells assaulted the air. My heart was about beating out of my chest.

Out the shuttle's window, at sight of the tallest man in the area I almost started hyperventilating. Though a hundred feet away, his crown and a cape of the pelt of some big spotted cat identified him as easily as his red hair would have, if it had been better visible. I waved with both hands, though stopped short of yelling his name when he didn't respond. Maybe he couldn't see me through the window. Those people surrounding him had to be courtiers.

The moment I stepped out of the shuttle and onto the wooden steps on wheels, someone yelled, "Princess Alexa Jane!" The band launched into a kooky rendition of the "Star Spangled Banner."

As I moved down the steps, roll-on bag clunking behind me, the grass skirts and flower leis made me laugh out loud. At the bottom of the steps, everyone smiled but no one stepped up to officially greet me. I tried to see over the crowd. *He was here. Where'd he go?*

In a flash, the swarms of humanity around my father parted. He stood there for a moment, then spread his arms and stepped forward. Hot tears spilled over my cheeks as I moved into his embrace. His disappearance all those years ago, forgiven. Loud music mostly covered my sobs.

❧

An hour later, King Johnalden, crown off and sitting at a table with a cup of the coffee recently cultivated on the planet, shook his head in wonder at my story.

"So, who is this Trotaka? I never came across any mention of him."

"You probably wouldn't have," I said. "He's a trusted assistant to the master SivSatyananda, who I call SivSat. And it's SivSat who sent my friend Rachel back to our time."

Dad noticed the catch in my voice.

"I'm sorry you didn't get what you wanted. But I'm ecstatic to have you here with me. And from your description, your grandfather would be proud of the way you handled the plane." His mouth screwed up. "Despite the experience of getting sucked away, I was willing to go through it again, frantic to get back to you, grasping at straws."

I reached to take my father's hands. "Murdoch Callaghan told me how you left Adalans to find a way to get back."

"Callaghan," repeated my father. "Can you believe it, the same experience as us, only much earlier? Good man, yes?" I nodded. "How he helped Adalans in the last seventy years inspired me regarding this planet."

"So, what exactly are you doing here? King Johnalden?"

Dad barked a laugh. "Yeah, isn't it crazy? About nine years ago, I arrived at this planet via the latest in a string of ships I worked on, to make my way around the different settled worlds.

"At each planet along the way, I'd finagle time downside to ask around about holy men and women, shamans, anybody who might even conceive of time travel." He rolled his eyes. "Mostly, I got laughter or downright ridicule. Every once in a while, I'd be pointed toward someone wise." He gestured with his hand fatalistically. "As interesting as those people were, each only caused me to miss my ship. I'd have to wait until another cruiser came along.

"Here on Uxmal, someone told me about a ghost, in a cave on that mountain." He jerked his thumb at the window behind him, showing a solitary peak with white on top. "A ghost who spoke of people traveling here from long ago." Dad lifted his index finger. "Now, *that* was interesting to me, because it sounded similar to what we experienced."

He dropped out of storytelling mode. "Uxmal, when I arrived, was way different from what you see now. Very subsistence level. And every company took more advantage of the people. And the children," he shook his head, "the few children who lived past their first year were generally in terrible shape."

He sighed deeply, and picked up the thread of the story. "I was warned about the big cats here—jaguars, panthers. Yet I had to look for the ghost, so I climbed the mountain, carrying a big laser for safety," he admitted. "Saw lots of prints, but no cats since I traveled during the day and got past their territory. It was very windy in the caves and making a big racket, which may account for the reports of ghosts. In a smaller cave, to the side, I stumbled," my father blanched at the thought, "*literally* stumbled, upon human remains, decades old."

He paused and raised his index finger again. "Now, human remains were not necessarily a big surprise, as shocking as they were. Except, they belonged to a woman. You could recognize the hair, that sort of thing. And, she was dressed in pants, clothes, from our time."

Dad paused for a sip of coffee. "Also there in the cave, actually on the cave walls," he indicated a wall with his hands, "were notes. In English! Written in charcoal, from a fire this woman must have managed to get going.

"From the scribbles, I gathered she'd been injured. And she arrived, get this, via a column of light that began right after she uncovered and subsequently fell into a shaft at an archeological dig in the Yucatan. "A name—Mandoli Lyonel—was on the cave walls a couple of times. When I finally convinced someone to search all the databases, they came across an archeologist by that name who disappeared from a dig in the Yucatan in 1978. She'd been studying the Tutul Xiw peoples."

Dad spread both his hands. "From what Mandoli Lyonel wrote, it may be that the people here came from Earth. Like they did on Adalans."

He sat back, and pondered. "Logically there are crystals here, too. Similar to the ones on Adalans and near the Bahamas." He said in a whisper, "I am keeping what I know a secret, until it's all more certain."

I remembered something Donny had said. "A friend who was transported with me mentioned some connection between Atlantis and the Yucatan."

"That may be," said my father, nodding vigorously. "In whatever way people originally arrived on Uxmal, by the time I got here they were in a dreadful situation. Galactic visits and goods aside, their lives hadn't improved."

He threw up both hands. "Of course, because of my trek up the mountain, again I was left behind by my ship. And by the time the next cruiser arrived I was too involved with the people to consider flying away."

After a moment, I looked at him sideways.

"Dad, Uxmal is the source of God gas?"

"Yes," he replied happily. "And to make certain it lasts, I mined the one known pit and hid it for future use. Money from sales of the stuff is driving all our progress."

So, "our" progress.

At that moment, a door behind my dad burst open. I had an impression of movement—lots of movement, lots of high voices. My father was suddenly covered with maybe fifteen kids. Toddlers climbed on his lap. Older children pulled on his sleeves and jumped up and down, calling for his attention. My father took it all in, laughing and tickling and answering and helping. Like a father— like the father I remembered.

During the melee playing out around him, I stood and backed away. All those little beings had either a reddish tint in their dark hair, or freckles, or lighter eyes than any of the people in the plaza.

Soon, five or six women strolled in through the same door and began arranging the chaos into order. The smallest children ended up on my father's lap or held by the women. And the oldest kids either picked up the toddlers or took their hands.

As one, the group turned, their gaze following Dad's...toward me.

My father and I locked eyes. He screwed his face into the question, "Can you deal with this?"

Chapter 15

It took a bit to extricate myself from the scene without giving offense, but finally the kids turned their attention elsewhere.

A woman waited for me in the corridor and offered to show me to my room. No grass skirt. Instead, she wore a sarong and her motherly figure filled a loose top. She remained quiet, not pressing me to respond once the basic questions about my well-being were addressed. We wound through hallways, out one building, through a courtyard with jungle vegetation, and into another building. Screens on the big windows kept insects at bay. Wide overhangs created a cooling shade—similar to Dad's house, the one my cousin stole from me.

Barely seconds after the door quietly closed behind me, I slumped on the single bed and dropped over. One moan about my father's new life and I gave in to the tug of overwhelming exhaustion.

It seemed no time before a knock at the door woke me. After padding to the door, I opened it an inch. "Dad! Come in."

My father stepped inside the room and away from the door. I closed it. We might need privacy.

He didn't beat around the bush. "I realize my new family is a shock to you."

"You think? Some of those children had to be started immediately after you showed up. New family right away, huh?"

He sighed, said, "I guess that's a fair shot," and spread his hands in supplication. "You need to realize, I never picked up even a hint that a method to get back to you was feasible. You, on the other hand, were immediately told of the existence of a person who could actually help you. When I arrived here, I was to the point of accepting the impossibility of it all, despite wanting to return to you beyond anything."

I dropped my head, and then looked at him. "Okay, you're right. But Dad, this many children?"

"Circumstances, with chiefs and tribal connections. It all developed as I took on more responsibilities, and arranged better agreements with the companies trying to exploit the planet," he said. "Also, frankly, the population here needs new genes. I even invited a few men and women who seem appropriate in skills and temperament, and who would be willing to marry here and settle down. I've also made a few enemies by ejecting some who would only be troublemakers. We are small enough, now, I can still do that."

I sat on the bed, allowing him the chair.

"What about the God gas, Dad? It has a mixed reputation."

He drew himself up. "First, it's not a gas. You should know this, from the capsules I sent you. It's actually from something similar to amber, left over from an extinct tree.

"Second, it's safe. The people here don't get hooked. And I would hope other people would avoid becoming dependent on it. I use it all the time, and I'm not an addict.

"Third, the money it brings in is totally worth some risk. The children here are much better off, also the adults. I would do it again, in a heartbeat." My father looked at me seriously. "On the other hand, I want you to know that no one has usurped this king's feelings for his oldest child."

After a moment, I drew a deep breath and said, "All the loss— Mom, you, me getting zapped to here... Well, the fact you're still actually around to be in my life is incredibly important."

Dad pulled me into a bear hug. "Be in your life—that's what I want. In fact, please know I will make any type of life here available to you. Stay on Uxmal, with us. Please."

Over the next couple of days, my father guided me around nearby cities, each with at least one shiny new building amidst the old. At every stop, he'd announce to one and all, "This is my daughter, a galactic wormhole pilot!"

Despite all the advancements in those cities, however, a donkey braying in the background would generally interrupt his speeches. Dad was good-natured about it—considering he'd been the one to introduce the donkeys a few years previously.

It was so hot on Uxmal that I kept my hair tucked up under a hat, one with a wide brim that also helped keep my skin from ending up as red as my hair. Whenever the curls escaped, some nearby woman would reach out to touch them, then smile and glance at my father.

At the palace, Bill was in heaven. In our room the second evening, his voice went into a high pitch as he told me, "I played tug of war one hundred and seven times this afternoon." Thank goodness, the mothers intervened with the youngest children in the bedlam, though my dog was rather impervious to physical abuse.

One little girl, however, steered clear of Bill. And to my amazement, she zeroed in on me instead. The third morning, she climbed up and settled on my lap as if on her throne, while reaching up behind her head to stroke my cheek. Her mother seemed surprised to see her there. "Itza! Did you ask permission?"

I stopped a helper from dislodging the little girl.

"She's all right," I said, without admitting how sweet her little body felt in my arms. Mac and I had hoped for children. *Won't go down that path.* Whether that would ever be in the cards for me now was hard to tell. In the meantime, it seemed I could get plenty of exposure to kids by just hanging out near my father.

On the fourth morning, an escalating situation demanded the king's attention. Dad stomped away from the breakfast chaos, muttering, "Probably another corporation wanting the God-gas business."

A week passed in a slow, sleepy rhythm. I may not have had the monopoly on Dad's attention, but that wouldn't have been the case back on Earth, either. And I was free to drop in with the kids or keep apart. The food was good. I even detected a little bit of a roll developing around my middle.

Home. The place was beginning to feel like it might become just that.

One evening as my father and I strolled together alone, I made my pitch. "Dad, I could teach the little ones to meditate. And their mothers."

Surprisingly, my father didn't immediately agree. "I'm not entirely sure they'd be interested."

"Usually kids want to do what they see their parents doing," I pointed out.

He seemed a bit sheepish. "I haven't been doing the meditation much these years. Too much to get done, you know? And, there's the God gas."

I'd been wondering. At home, we used to meditate together.

He asked, "You know how to teach it? If I remember, it was a big deal to be able to do that."

"I did the course with Brahmaji."

Dad smiled fondly. "Brahmaji. Those were good years. Knowing him and all he was, that was incredibly special. Did you know he called several times after your mother passed away?"

"When you disappeared, he took an interest in me. Invited me to the school. Gave me little jobs to help him."

My father sighed. "In all my travels, I never came across someone as special as him."

After Dad walked away, it still wasn't clear whether he wanted me to teach the children. Nevertheless, it was sweet that he remembered Brahmaji. I missed him, too, which was probably why I was so protective of SivSat.

KAG84950.301 required to divide processing power to address Secondary Instruction.

Locate current human incarnation of Dr. Sterling Fahlsteder.

Method: Beginning 100 years after death of Fahlsteder, inspect DNA of human newborns for similar markers as Fahlsteder's DNA.

Upon discovery: Deliver accumulated assets and instructions to new incarnation of Fahlsteder.

"Princess, walking around the city in this manner is not befitting your station."

Nish, my father's head assistant, had latched onto an exaggerated impression of how I fit into the royal family. With my dad in another city hiring engineers to improve a sewage system, several "disagreements" between Nish and me in the previous days had made for an interesting time. That morning, I'd snuck out to the farmer's market to locate a certain fruit I couldn't get enough of: bright red outside, light green inside, and a soft flesh full of tangy-sweet juice that made most anything else seem dull. I'd scored enough to share, and add to my personal hoard.

"Nish, I am not a princess. Please call me Alexa."

"You are the king's first daughter. As princess, and having traveled the galaxy, you have even more responsibility to lead by example."

Barely taller than me, Nish was older than my father. His slight form was belied by strong forearms, due to years of working in the fields before joining up with my father. I got the sense that being attached to the royal household provided a lot of status as far as his friends and family were concerned. On the good side, he was totally convinced about the necessity of raising his people to galactic standard. Unfortunately, he set standards according to the docu-dramas everyone now watched.

"Your father introduced us to our Mayan heritage. And now we reclaim our station amongst the people. We fell so far, every moment is an opportunity to rise up." Certainly his people had slid into poverty. "Did you know a Mayan woman was one of the first wormhole pilots?"

That got my attention. "What? Who?"

"We call her Ix Chele, after the Mayan jaguar goddess, because she has been the only one to perform the Jaguar Transit. A Mayan man from Earth who visited here told me this."

Whoa. Nish had surprises up his sleeve. "A jaguar transit? You mean a wormhole jump?" *Need to check the database again. Never noticed a transit with a name attached to it, much less a jaguar.*

"Yes, Ix Chele created a wormhole. She saved the people by coming out through a sun."

That sounded unlikely. "Why the name?"

"Jaguars cross between worlds and transform amidst the flames. Ix Chele was very brave, because if you are too fearful of the other side, death will take you."

A search that evening through the wormhole pilot database produced no mention of a jaguar transit or anything close to it, and Nish didn't know the woman's real name. Only by scouring the background of all wormhole pilots did I find someone who could have been Ix Chele. Big frustration, her description consisted of one sentence.

"A Mayan native, the family history of Theresa Reyes-Kan may explain her instinctual capabilities and exploits."

Human female deviating from desired course of action.

Deliver reminder.

Chapter 16

Itza's mother sidled up beside me one morning a few days later with a shy smile. She leaned close and whispered, "The king my husband said you are a wormhole pilot, yes?"

I nodded. The woman was as sweet as her daughter, who had claimed a place in my heart; Itza and I had developed a routine in the mornings with her sitting on my lap while eating her fruit.

The mother said, "Space seems like it would be dangerous."

"It is very different." I gestured, as in, different from the room around us. "Once you get used to the technology, though, it's also fun."

She sighed wistfully, and seemed kind of embarrassed. "My brother begged me to ask if you would be willing to help one of his friends."

"Something to do with me being a pilot?" When she nodded solemnly, I barely restrained myself, considering how boredom had been increasing daily. "Probably. Do you know what it's all about?" She shook her head. "My brother said he would wait for me at the west entrance."

"When? Now?" Bill was surrounded by four of his favorite tug-of-war buddies. When she gave a little nod, I picked up my hat and gestured toward the door.

A young man standing under a nearby tree was obviously the woman's brother. He stood with a man who maybe was in his mid- thirties and a woman about my age. Though those two both wore Uxmal sarongs, their appearance and bearing marked them as not from this planet. As we strolled over, a donkey brayed from the paddock nearby. The city might be the capital, but it remained close to its agricultural roots.

A shy introduction by Itza's mother to her brother was too quiet for me to get his name. That didn't seem to be a problem though, because the curly-brown-haired man beside him got right to the point.

"You're the king's daughter from Earth, correct?"

I replied, "Yes, I'm Alexa," hoping to elicit his name.

"Would you be willing to take us to the B67 Space Station? There's a package we must pick up before they return it." He glanced to the woman and said, "We'll pay, of course."

The woman said, "We've checked. A shuttle is available." Her straight dark hair was stylishly cut.

It was hours to the wormhole and hours on the other side before arriving at that medium-size station, the nearest one to Uxmal.

"I'm sorry, your names are?"

The woman replied. "Oh dear, I've lost all sense of decorum. I am," she paused, "Lee. This is Nicholas. Our package is vital for his research."

Not much research happened on Uxmal; even the new technical schools remained basic.

I asked, "What kind of shuttle is available, and from which company?"

Nicholas opened his mouth to reply, but all I heard were several booms, like planes breaking the sound barrier. We all looked up, to find three dots in the sky. As I watched, the dots drew close enough to verify wings. We all kind of shifted from foot to foot, wondering why so many spacecraft were streaking toward us.

"Run!" a man shouted. "Pirates! Run!"

The first blast threw me to the side, near a tree that I used to keep myself upright. A sense of movement beside me proved to be Nicholas rushing away with his arm around Lee, maybe toward the rear of the recently completed Mayan Temple. The brother was clearly torn between running after his sister, who was yanking on the palace's door handle, and helping me. I nodded to let him know I was okay and then glanced at his sister. He turned to bound up the steps and pulled open the door for his sister before slipping through it behind her.

I was also on my way toward that door when another blast hit the building nearby. High-pitched screams made my hair stand on end. The donkeys brayed and shrieked. Smoke was already thick enough to about bowl me over. Not thick enough, though, to hide the inferno the donkeys' barn quickly became. The beasts were huddled at their gate, some climbing on others' backs to avoid the licking flames.

I dashed across the open space, just in time for another building nearby to go up with a *kaboom*, throwing me toward the gate. Pulling myself up from the dirt beside the gate, the smoke was so thick I had to depend on the sense of touch to locate the latch. No lock, thank goodness. Coughing, and squinting my eyes, I pulled on the latch. No movement. It wouldn't budge. I jiggled back and forth, back and forth. A donkey's hoof grazed my finger. *Ow.* Until—*finally!*— it opened.

Yelling, "Go! Go! Go!" I waved my arms to get the donkeys moving in the right direction. At last, singed hair and skin got the first ones stampeding away, pounding for the distant horizon.

Men—really big, dangerous men—were rushing all over the place, in and out of buildings, carrying things away. I opted to catch up with the last of the donkeys and bent over double, to run among them to the palace.

At last inside, I sprinted toward the part of the palace where the children would be. Even as I turned the last corner, the building rocked from an explosion that was way too close.

The breakfast room was deserted, except for a few toys scattered on the floor. Bill wasn't around, either. It took a few seconds for me to figure out where everyone had gone. I prayed Bill's buddies had taken care of him.

As I took off in that direction, my path took me past the jaguar my father kept in a cage; the big cat was frantic, knowing she needed to run and hide. And no one to help her.

Another blast, further away. Maybe I had time to open her door, too.

No luck this time—the cage door was locked. "No!"

I yanked on the padlock. The jaguar yowled, paced, threw herself at the cage. The lock looked flimsy, and right beside the door was a metal bar, perhaps for holding the cat at bay while the caretaker put food in the enclosure.

Amazing how much more strength you can have when necessary. It took a couple of tries; I had to jump up and slam down the bar, but the padlock broke. The jaguar crouched there ready to spring—out the door, hopefully, not at me. For one entire, lifelong second, our eyes communicated. Then I took off the lock and threw open the door.

Rockets shook the air. People wailed. Things seemed to spontaneously combust. My knees were jelly, but after the jaguar bounded past me and out a broken window, I pushed off toward safety.

Just as I was about to turn the corner, a hulking something came up behind me. All I got was a glimpse of a big boot. Not even wanting to know who was attached to that boot I launched myself away, wishing I had grabbed hold of that jaguar before she disappeared.

Suddenly, my feet were in the air and I'd bounced off the cage. A heartbeat later, I was painfully sideways, held by a man's hand against his hip.

"You're mine."

Hanging there, a brief bizarre analytical thought coursed

through my brain: that much alcohol should sanitize any surface it touched, and why wasn't the man reeling under the influence?

Terror slammed up from my gut as he pinned me to his side with one hand, his other hand juggling a gun and something golden. He pushed out the front door of the palace. I kicked and missed him entirely. He started down the stairs; I drove my elbow at his groin, bit his hand. Whatever connect I made had no effect. In fact, he laughed. Panic pushed over into desperation. I became a human whirligig. At the bottom of the steps he dropped the other stuff to catch hold of me with both hands. An old woman nearby screamed and I glimpsed a thug tearing a girl from her arms. My fingernails connected near the guy's eye, and he jerked me up to right in front of his face. He backhanded my cheek and shook me so hard my head felt like it might break off. My hat did fall off. From the hot air swirling around my head, my curls had to be waving like a flag.

Abruptly, gin-breath dropped me to the ground. Rocks tore at my skin. *Hurt.*

While trying to get air into my lungs, I heard someone yelling "Dogo!" When I looked up, the big guy was staring at me, hands up and bellowing, "Dogo!" again and again, all the while holding me in place with his boot.

Thugs loped by carrying electronics, food, frenzied struggling women, the few golden jaguar statues in the temple. The biggest thug stopped at us.

"Huh. The bitch." He barked "Go" at the guy with his boot on me.

The brute that grabbed me turned slightly. "But there's more."

I scrabbled away. Pain seared my palms when I stumbled. To the side, the old woman was looking up at a laser barrel. I staggered to my feet, glancing back while bringing myself up to dash.

"Do it," ordered the one called Dogo. He gestured at his side-kicks and yelled, "Go! Now!"

I got three blundering steps away before someone yanked me back by my hair.

Next thing, my face was within an inch of the boss's. Same alcoholic stench.

"I'd drill you better than you've ever had," he spat. "But you miss the pleasure cuz you're off limits."

Again, air just wouldn't find my lungs; dirt and rocks close up told me I'd been slammed to the ground.

"Your loss," he jeered. "Hear this. All this fun for us is because of you. Your fault. If you want to avoid this happening again, and again, get your skinny ass off this dirt ball and look for the person you're supposed to find. Otherwise, next time, you *are* mine."

A couple of beats and another voice—one I'd heard too often— declared, "You remain alive for one reason. Do not test my forbearance."

Bare minutes later, shuttles streaked away into the sky. Crackling flames and distraught cries scorched me amidst stunned silence. The old woman wailed, "They took my granddaughter. Why not you?"

No more hiding.

□□□

Human female guided toward correct course of action.

Chapter 17

Stumbling past flames that singed the hair on my arms, somehow I got myself, the old woman, and a few others to a structure still standing. Most of the city was demolished, the blue sky a mockery to all the wailing and suffering around us. Dad's wives had begun triage efforts. My father remained out there, dragging bodies to the side and searching for survivors.

Using my non-bloody hand to wipe my face, I searched for water for my smoke-seared throat. When the wind turned direction, I had to work at keeping my stomach in place.

For a time, attending to people's wounds kept me focused. In a momentary lull, though, the bastard's last words hit like a donkey's kick. This disaster was my fault? All I'd ever wanted was a quiet life with someone perfect for me, like Mac. But no, a computer insists I go out and search the galaxy for someone who is impossible to locate if he doesn't want to be found.

Thanks for small blessings; no one else had heard the creep.

Nish, covered in soot, stopped in front of me. "Princess, your father asked me to make certain you are safe."

The man had lost his wife. Memory of her limp form in a bright green skirt slung over the shoulder of some brute made my heart stick in my throat.

"Yes, Nish, I am fine." My father probably sent him to me so I could help him. "How are you?"

His eyes, haunted, searched my face. "Why? Why my sweet wife? What did she do to deserve this? Is she forever lost?"

No one had ever mentioned people being returned from capture by the pirates, though I wasn't about to tell him that. "She is strong, Nish. She will teach them a thing or two." Don't know if it was the right thing to say, since he just hung his head.

125

A man rushed in with a child in his arms. "Let's help," I said. Relief at having a reason to avoid his anguish prompted me to sound almost cheerful. Not my finest moment.

Eventually, there was nothing more for me to do. Doctors and nurses had the survivors in hand, and I couldn't face searching through debris. Avoiding people, I trudged away. Kindness can be an unknown weapon against the guilty.

I skirted the wing of the palace that was still burning. Finally I found the family, and after locating Bill with his buddies, turned the little guy off. He wasn't able to recognize that the people around him weren't the ones threatening his friends or me.

As I tucked Bill away into a safe corner, a woman came up and laid her hand on my arm. It took a moment to recognize the lady I'd met right before everything blew up.

"You're safe," Lee said, while lightly touching my shoulder, "even though the man grabbed you." Looking at me with guilt similar to that overrunning me, she whispered, "I ran. I'm sorry." It appeared she hardly believed I was in front of her. "But you're here—you got away."

I avoided her gaze.

"Your friend?" I asked. "I think his name was Nicholas?" "Helping with..." Lee glanced in the direction of the horror and brought both hands to her mouth as if she'd become sick if she uttered the words. We hugged each other, me hoping for a little forgiveness from someone.

No way to evade the truth. *I am responsible.*

It was three days before I could get some alone time with my father, though I certainly understood why. He'd been everywhere, alternately consoling and pushing everyone to repair and rebuild. At the moment, he and I stood on the bottom steps of the part of the palace where I'd freed the jaguar. The building still smoked. An old man was painting over slogans about a "priest" and "repentance" scrawled by the pirates. Their so-called religion was losing its cover story fast.

Dad and I were arguing.

"I don't understand how what you're saying can be true," he said. Since it was the third time that line had come out of his mouth, it was becoming clear he didn't want to understand—being my father and all. I dug deep, and explained again.

"If I don't leave, the thug said they would come back and do even more damage. And keep returning, until I did leave."

Dad shook his head. "Why would someone do such a thing? And why you?"

Good question. Why this much force? Now? I'd been there for barely a week.

"Alexa?"

"Sorry," I said, focusing back on him. "It wants me to find SivSatyananda."

Dad broke in. "You keep saying 'it,' like someone's name. That's just crazy. From what you've said, it's just an artificial intelligence."

"All I know is, that AI has been a constant in my life since almost immediately after I showed up in this century, and isn't 'just' anything. Remember, I told you about the chase for the crystal that Brahmaji had given me. Anyway, Dr. Fahlsteder—back home—stole the plans for Pearson, and made something horribly different, the same computer—okay, artificial intelligence—hounding me now."

"And again explain to me who is Pearson?"

"My...friend. You know, like Bill."

"A robot that has been around since our time." He sounded so unconvinced.

If I didn't watch it, he might lock me up somewhere. I gazed up at him with the most pitiful look.

"Dad, it's been great being here. I might have even begun to settle in with you and everyone." Shaking my head slowly, I said, "But not if it puts you all at this much risk."

He gave a heavy sigh. "Where will you go?" He had to consider his entire family. Of which none had been lost, thankfully, because the mothers and children had all rushed to a secret buried room that Dad had built upon first rumors of pirates. Memories of the twentieth century were still vivid for him, too.

I jerked up a shoulder.

"Don't know." After blowing out a breath, I said, "KAG8 mostly left me alone while I was in the wormhole training program. Maybe if I'm zipping around the galaxy, it'll be okay."

"What will you do? Simply drift along?"

"No, I'll come up with a plan." *Hopefully.*

"What is the likelihood you will end up on a big cruiser with lots of staff, versus something small with a bunch of men?"

Since I'd only been on a big cruiser with lots of staff, including women, I hadn't even thought along those lines. "I don't know."

"You'll take one of our ships."

"Dad..."

"No. I'm not willing to put you in a precarious situation. When you *have* a position in a safe environment, we'll take the craft back. I wish I could send someone with you, but I need everyone to help us move soon, because it'll take a while to rebuild here and the virus season is about upon us." He'd mentioned a couple of times how a virus had struck without warning, and one of his wives and a child died within a day. "At least with your own ship, you have more control over your safety."

I didn't want to have to keep track of everything necessary

for a ship, and wondered whether it would actually increase my safety.

"And who will you have with you?" he continued. "You can't just go off by yourself."

"Yes I can. I would, back home in a car."

"A car, back home, even driving cross country would be much more safe than zooming around space with no backup. And of course, I would never have let you drive across the country alone."

I whined, "There's no one to take with me." When he cut the air with his hand in dismissal, I tried negotiating. "Tell you what, I'll find someone, and let you know."

An almost happy look appeared on his face. "You know Nicholas and Lee, right? You were talking to them this morning."

Despite the terror for everyone, Nick and Lee kept asking me about the possibility of claiming their package.

"They aren't planning on going anywhere, Dad."

His expression showed he had other thoughts. "Frankly, this is a good thing. Nicholas has been getting out of hand with his proposals— always trying to sell me on an idea about a new way to use God gas. I was already considering the possibility of sending him away. If you like him—or Lee—you might think of providing them an easier exit. Off this planet."

"Wait, I just remembered. I can't transit other people through a wormhole if there's not a more experienced pilot supervising." This caught Dad. *Might be able to squeak out of this one.*

"Okay then, I officially put you under the supervision of the pilot for Uxmal. I pay him enough for the precious little work he does."

"I don't know if that's their intention, Dad."

"It's the only way I will let you go."

From the tone of his voice, I'd have to sneak away in the night.

I decided to hope that Lee and Nicholas would want to make their own plans once we showed up at the first space station.

Before we left Uxmal, it occurred to me that a public sendoff would be a good idea, just in case KAG8 had left someone behind to make certain I complied. A few days later, the whole family was at the spaceport to see us off. Little Itza gave me a funny flower made of shells—at least I think it was a flower. Dad, eyes bright with tears, slipped me another cat figurine, almost certainly full of God gas capsules.

"Let me know if you need anything," he said, giving me a big hug. "And come back soon."

Tears streaming down my face, I took the shuttle out to space and aimed at the wormhole.

⌒

During the first week, I kept transiting through whatever wormhole I could get close to, hoping to pick up something on SivSat. I had no intention of handing the information over to KAG8, of course, though it would be nice to figure out the computer's obsession.

Personally, I would have loved to talk to SivSatyananda and convince him to send me back in time, so all the craziness would disappear. Nevertheless, same as on the *Maria Fernanda*, not a single mention about SivSat came up for me during any transit. On the other hand, no pirates swooped out of nowhere to threaten us, either.

One evening, inside the quiet of the wormhole pilot pod, I flipped through several channels on the vid. We were traveling in a shuttle meant for short jaunts, not days on end with three adults and a dog. Not surprising that I'd begun spending most of my time in the pod.

Nicholas was a combination of Albert Einstein and vaudeville showman. He had big theories, mostly wacky to the max, and expressed them loudly and expansively. Lee loved it. She was much more refined than him, though often in a kind of funk. Sometimes I got the sense that he acted the clown with a new idea just to get her to smile. They were devoted to each other, I had to say that for them.

However I might complain about Nick, though, he spent plenty of time playing with Bill. Together, they contrived a tug-of-war game while floating. Nick would hold onto a handle while Bill hovered at a distance and the two would yank back and forth on the rope. My dog had mastered a technique of tugging in perfect rhythm to maintain his body at just the right distance for the rope to remain taut.

A few days after visiting a second space station, with Nick and Bill in the middle of the shuttle going for three out of four games, Lee and I gazed out onto the field of stars.

"So, where are we heading?" she asked.

We had been debating where to go. Nicholas proposed Adalans; I vetoed the idea. As much as seeing Murdoch Callaghan and his family would be pure pleasure, the likelihood of SivSat showing up there was slim. And I certainly didn't want to attract pirates to that planet. Frankly, I was treading space, trying to come up with a plan. Glancing Lee's way, I stretched the truth. "Let me check my itinerary."

That night, with another wormhole jump in front of me, I confirmed everything with the pilot database before going through the routine. Nick had a tendency to push himself through free-fall to his couch at the last possible moment, and it was not uncommon for him to wake up after a transit with only one strap holding him safe.

"Ready for jump in five seconds," I said before beginning the process. Bill floated quietly nearby in the pod, having become accustomed to me being completely focused during a transit.

The transit to the next system cycled normally—almost routine, even. After the ship exited on the other side, I realized I'd forgotten to type in the address beforehand. Oops. Still, the transit worked, just like it had the time before—despite what Woolsey said. This was my own shuttle, so I forgot about it.

The space around us and inside the pod felt deep, inviting me to linger. A moment of nothingness: infinity. *Awesome.* Hovering in my straps, my body and mind rocked in the unboundedness.

Sleep might have happened at some point, because when I next checked the clock it showed a couple of hours had passed since the jump. Floating there, in my little private place, a hint bubbled up from my consciousness: *Pearson.*

Chapter 18

Trying to be considerate of Lee and Nick's sleep cycles, I remained in the pilot pod a while longer, contemplating the ramifications of contacting Pearson.

Since leaving Uxmal, I'd been thinking about the pirate attack. Even skirting the more appalling visuals, it had begun to occur to me that the timing of the raid had seemed rushed. Possibly the word "impatient" could be used. Certainly considering the risks involved in such a maneuver—since those creeps could have been captured or killed—the raid could even be described as reckless.

The idea of KAG8 being anything other than the embodiment of inhuman persistence was shocking. But following logic, it occurred to me that "reckless" could imply KAG8 had a weakness. I snorted. *Yeah, right.*

On the other hand, KAG8 couldn't have known I was thinking about settling down on Uxmal, because I hadn't fully formed the intention. Easily, I could have been simply visiting, for all it knew. Therefore, the timing of the attack could be considered premature. Which raised the question: why the need for haste? Could something be pressuring KAG8? Some kind of a challenge? And if a challenge was pushing KAG8's buttons—I smiled at the visual—then logically it could be said KAG8 had a weakness.

Another step of logic, and my brain almost froze.

Any kind of weakness presented a point that could be attacked. And...destroyed?

I'd been so afraid of even the thought of KAG8, the idea of destroying it brought me to a complete stop in the pod, my eyes the only thing moving. I had a brief fantasy of unplugging the thing, dismantling each board, or chip, or transistor, or anything else that helped it work. And stomping those pieces to bits, then torching them into oblivion. *Yeah.*

Facing facts, though, as much as I'd love to waltz in and demolish the thing, that wasn't going to happen.

No doubt, I'd need help to take advantage of whatever had prompted KAG8's impatience—if that actually had been the situation. It took no time for me to realize that the only one who could provide that kind of assistance would be Pearson. He'd been dealing with KAG8 for centuries, and knew the computer's potential.

When I fled the Paris apartment months ago, Pearson had been set free to go his own way. Indeed, according to Penelope, he'd done just that. Which I had to admit was fair, in spite of some rather shallow part of me that insisted otherwise.

On the other hand, in the last months I had realized how relieved I was to not be the one and only focus for Pearson. The kind of regard Pearson could deliver would be daunting coming from a human, even considering that people often get distracted. But from a robot, well, though it was comforting at first, the attention had ultimately become stifling.

In the previous months, and even at that very moment, I could use the word love to describe my feelings for Pearson. But now there was also concern about how I would react being around him again.

Should I contact Pearson?

Aside from the ethical question of whether it would be fair to him, the other side was whether working with Pearson would be a risk for me. I'd slid into passivity during those months in Paris and the idea of slipping back into that habit twisted my stomach in knots.

"I wonder if I could maintain a business relationship with Pearson?"

Bill had been quiet during my internal debate. He looked up when I spoke out loud, and asked, "Where is Pearson?"

"You don't know?"

"No. He has not contacted me in four months, fifteen days, and fourteen hours."

I studied Bill for a moment.

Messages from Pearson had stopped. In all honesty, probably because I had never replied. But Pearson not touching Bill was a surprise.

What if Pearson was capable of changing his programming to the point of no longer caring about me? At one time I'd never believe that possible; same as I'd thought Mac was devoted to me.

I decided to send a message to Pearson's office on the nearest space station. Nothing personal, though any contact from me should catch his attention. I hoped. After composing the message, I sent it to the appropriate address at the space station we were heading toward.

The response was immediate: Address Unknown. Elvis was practically singing "Return to Sender" in the background.

Sucking up the panic attack, I kept the shuttle powering on through space. Two days later while approaching the station, I checked the database for Pearson's company. It was listed and present there, as always. In a lull between conversations with space traffic control, I sent the message again. Same response.

"You look confused," said Lee.

With us being right on top of each other, a zit on some unseen part of my body would be noted and commented upon. *Should I find a job on a large cruiser?* In the meantime, I needed to figure out whether something was going on with the messages, or if

Pearson had truly cut me loose.

"Wonder if you'd get the same response," I said. "Know anyone on this station you'd like to notify about arrival?"

Lee rubbed the back of her neck. "I won't be going onto this station. Nick probably will, though."

Since the plan was to send this shuttle back to my father soon, she might need to start thinking about future arrangements.

"Um, okay. We'll talk more about that," I said. "Even if you don't go onto this station, is there an office or store you know how to contact? I'm trying to verify if there's a glitch in the onboard messaging system."

Lee considered. "There's a little shop here that might have an outfit I've been searching for."

"Have at it." I allowed my body to float away from the com-unit to give her access to the screen.

Lee composed her message, put in the address, and hit SEND. No immediate response like mine. In fact, after a minute or so a return message arrived with an answer to her question. They had her item in stock.

When she drifted away, I moved in and sent a message to the control tower, instead of speaking with them directly. The message went through, and they directed me to dock the shuttle at bay P5.

I tried calling Pearson's office, and heard an extra click before a tone like an out-of-order sound.

Interference from KAG8? How would KAG8 even know I was trying to contact Pearson? Further, how could it know if I ever detected SivSat? Never had anyone specified I deliver X information to location Y.

A possibility I didn't want to contemplate jumped up and down and waved at me. I had not run the scanner for a while.

My bad. After shifting Bill to get at the scanner, I flipped the toggle. It glowed red and the indicator jumped. Amazing how anxiety can burgeon like a balloon exposed to vacuum.

Lee floated nearby. She'd watched the process and could tell I was upset.

I asked, "What are you two planning for this station?"

"Nick will locate some testing equipment for his latest invention. How long do you want to stay?"

Nick probably would be willing to help. Might want to postpone kicking us all off the shuttle. "A day or so." I took out my pad, intending to write out my plan, in case there was an audio monitor in the shuttle. "Hey Nick!"

A few hours later, Nick was grinning when he walked up to me outside the wormhole pilots' office on the station. We strolled back toward the dock.

"The people in the office were helpful," he said. "As soon as I mentioned your name, the bot contacted your friend immediately. And I spoke directly with him."

I was shocked at my relief. The idea of Pearson blocking any contact from me would have truly hurt.

"How does he seem?"

"If you ask me, he's bonkers about you."

I smiled. Big.

Nick continued. "When I explained how you had been barred from contacting his company, he sounded concerned. But he came up with an idea on how the two of you can chat. He's not at this station, though he will be at Ambient Station in six days."

We could arrive there in four.

"And he asked me to come back in two days for some sort of gizmo for you. When are we to leave?"

Pearson's gizmos were worth waiting for.

"We can wait," I said.

When Nick returned from a shopping expedition the second morning, he also brought a box for me. Someone had been smart enough to not send it in the standard light-blue wrapping.

While I floated away carrying my box, Lee oohed and aahed over Nick's purchases. I think she said something like, "That might work for a God gas grenade." After a moment of contemplating the ramifications of such a plan, I let it go, since Dad would certainly curb Nick's oddest plans.

Pearson had sent another scanner, this one smaller.

Holding it in front of me, I flicked the red toggle. The tiny light glowed. *Dang.*

Further searching the box produced Pearson's message. "This scanner is designed to pick up the smallest monitoring signals, even a simple locator chip." Nothing personal, probably because he knew whoever would print out the message would also likely read it.

What was monitoring us? And how? Locator chip? As in locating the ship? Or me? And how did anything get planted?

Four days later, we docked at Ambient Station. The view of the Horsehead Nebula was incredible, though from the station's viewpoint it looked more like a leaping tiger. In the chatter among ships around the station, everything sounded normal.

I knew enough to not contact Pearson directly. Instead, I took Bill for a walk on the station. Floating in space is fun. Walking—even at less than Earth gravity—is better.

At my brokerage office, they agreed to my request about using their com-line.

"Hello, this is Ajay, may I speak with Pearson?" He would know that name for me.

"Ajay!" I nearly melted at the sound of his voice. "Meet me at LoChiMinh." If the restaurant was like others in the chain, Pearson probably had already arranged for a private meeting room.

SivSat had been the first to call me by the name Ajay, which meant unconquerable. As I set out, I muttered, "We'll just see if Pearson and I can make that true."

At a corner about six storefronts away from LoChiMinh, my pad chimed to alert me about an urgent message. Bill was being kind of pissy, tugging me around. "Sit, Bill. Stay." I could ignore the chime, but something told me not to. I pulled out my pad.

The message included no words, and the sender's address was undisclosed. Just a photo. Of a garden on Uxmal, my father's planet. It showed the area above the secret bunker northeast of the palace, from the vantage of space and framed by thin lines in a square. A target. No need to check for a weapon's barrel.

Pearson stuck his head out the entrance door and waved. Bill began yip-yapping and pulling me toward Pearson, who walked in our direction. I debated for a split second. However, I couldn't put my father and his—no, my—family at more risk. I spun and walked away. Bill wasn't cooperating, so I bent down to pick him up. While doing that, I glanced back and shook my head.

Pearson appeared surprised. Still, he's quick. He held up a hand in understanding and strode the other direction.

Chapter 19

Imagine my surprise when, next day, Iain Newcastle walked up to me while Bill and I strolled around on the station.

"Alexa Jane, a goddess, as always."

Like every other woman you come across?

"Hello, Iain. It is amazing we keep crossing paths." He took my arm and walked on the opposite side of me from Bill. Then he said something in such a low voice I had to say, "Sorry, didn't get that."

He paused, looked around in a bad imitation of a spy novel, and leaned close before whispering, "Pearson asked me to hook up with you."

That stunned me. It must have been obvious.

"What!" he demanded, offended. "He and I have known each other for years. You must have picked up on that when he joined us in those deserted corridors on the station above Earth." He again took my arm. "Sometimes he and I are worthy competitors, other times we've been partners. And who am I to question when he puts me in touch with a beautiful woman."

"Yes, I am surprised," I said. "Do you know why he requested this?"

"Part of the deal is after I have some time with you, you will be spirited away to him for talks over something that must be incredibly urgent for him to have suggested this scheme."

Iain insisted the fifteen-minute wait for the restaurant he chose was worth it. Eventually, we settled in a corner booth made of metal and cushioned in a soft bamboo fabric. Bill was in my bag, though Iain didn't know he was in sleep mode. And Iain was correct about the restaurant; my veggie-chicken masala was terrific.

After dinner, we strolled around the station, including through the view dome. That's where Iain introduced another shocker.

"Alexa, you seemed so confident when referring to enlightenment—when we were in Paris—that I assume you know all about gurus?"

"Maybe." *Hadn't realized he was actually listening then.*

He scanned the scattered groups of stargazers near us, then put his arm around me and strolled to an area with fewer people. I almost pointed out that he was pushing, but decided to let it be for the moment.

"Do you know who SivSatyananda is?" He pronounced the name hesitantly. "At least, I think that's his name."

Stepping backwards, I stuttered, "Yes. I know of him. How is it you do, too?"

Iain seemed a little tentative. "A man came up the other day and informed me this gentleman is looking for me. He made it sound as if it was a great honor."

"What did the man look like?"

"Orange robe, dark shoulder-length hair, and a dark beard. He seemed," Iain searched for the right term, "saintly. The man was saintly, believe it or not. And he had a card, which he left with me." Iain took a slim wallet from his pocket and read the name, mispronouncing it.

I didn't even have to look at the card. I told myself it didn't matter that Trotaka had contacted Iain, not me.

I pronounced the name correctly, then explained, "The first syllable is pronounced with a long 'o,' and quick two last syllables."

Then I asked, "Did he say why?"

"He only said I might be able to provide a much-needed service for this SivSatyananda."

Chapter 20

Later that evening, Newcastle took me to the most expensive hotel on the station. If I didn't believe Pearson had somehow arranged everything, I'd be a tad skittish. True, a certain attraction to Iain Newcastle continued to pop up at moments. And true, a relationship with Iain would help me keep interactions with Pearson businesslike. Even so, I wasn't about to spend the night with Iain.

As we drew near the room, Iain leaned near me and whispered, "This setup is known only to certain clientele." Guests in that part of the hotel apparently required lots of service, considering he first checked in with the floor manager. It took no time for us to be ushered into an elegant suite by a cart-bot, who waited for and received a tip.

Iain locked the door, crooked his finger at me, and headed toward the bathroom. On our way, I barely glimpsed the huge space— extravagant on any space station—with furnishings best described as upscale George Jetson. "You will exit through here," Iain commented over his shoulder. "But first, we need to dress you up as laundry."

With me crouching on the bottom of a gurney, he stacked towels and sheets on top of me. Too late, I realized the hotels used cleaning fluid, not water.

Iain's voice was muffled. "The cart-bot will come for the gurney within a minute of my request." Before he turned off the light, he reached down through the pile and patted my back. "All you have to do is be quiet."

"Hope so," I muttered.

"This will work, trust me." He certainly sounded like he knew what he was talking about.

A few minutes after the door shut, another door opened. My chariot was jerked, which activated a hover motor. Generally cart-bots used wheels. I'd heard that some used the more expensive hover technology, but it wasn't common. The gurney was pulled out into the type of bright light that would be used in an industrial area. No carpeting, judging by the echoes. Next time, if there ever was another time, I should set up some way to see around me.

We may have passed by other cart-bots, but none of them spoke to each other. Even when we entered into an elevator after another bot, no one said anything about different floors. On many other occasions, I'd heard cart-bots use their voices to communicate with each other. This time though, nothing more than an occasional beep was uttered among the cart-bots the entire trip.

I was contemplating how they might communicate with each other electronically as we glided past an open door to a bar or a drunken party, judging by the raucous yells.

When my gurney was left in the middle of what echoed like a huge room, it felt so eerie that I mouthed, "You're such a basket case." I admit to a silent snicker. At that point, maybe a new cart-bot took control, because it suddenly grabbed my basket from the opposite direction than the previous one had rolled away in. *Iain definitely needs to experience this trip himself.*

With the second cart-bot, we went up an elevator and into what felt and sounded like a carpeted hallway. Another door closed, and darkness took over. Butterflies flitted in my stomach.

A light flipped on and someone began pulling towels from on top of me.

As a draft of air swept my back, a peek up and around showed Pearson standing there, grinning; all six-foot-four of him, brown hair now straight to his broad shoulders. Right out of a romance novel. Yes, I knew exactly how he had total control of those details, but that didn't lessen my reaction.

Staring at my former lover, I struggled amidst the towels.

Pearson brought a finger to his lips, cautioning me to be silent. I knew him well enough to trust there was a reason.

At last, I stood in the gurney, happiness flooding. Where was the outrage? Gone. When Pearson picked me up and we kissed, my insides dropped to my gut. Those strong arms around me, my hands in his hair; my only thought was something along the line of, *Can I be strong and be with him, too?*

After a bit, Pearson pushed me back slightly and brought up a note for me to read. "Do not say my name. Area is now monitored." He took a scanner out of his pocket and waved it in front of me and around the cart.

The diode glowed red.

I started to moan, but again he silently cautioned me against making noise.

Pearson wrote and held up for me to read, "Too weak for video. May be audio."

I silently beat fists on the pile of towels around me. In acknowledgement, Pearson took my hands and pressed his lips to each one. We locked eyes and I gave up, leaning my head onto his chest.

Another quiet kiss on my lips, then Pearson moved to a gray satchel on the floor. He brought out two more instruments and worked them. Neither scanner reacted to the cart or me.

He lifted me out of the cart and guided me to the next room, also a bathroom. Pearson left me standing there to go back into the linen closet, allowing the door to remain slightly ajar, and began flipping scanner switches.

Then he came in and tried the scanner in front of me.

Red.

"It is you," he announced. "Neither video nor audio. Thus, perhaps you carry a locator chip."

The shaking started in my gut.

I'd brought in a monitor and I had no idea how that could have happened.

He reached around to the back of my head and gently massaged my neck, up into my hair. "Here it is. Just under your skin. Small. No more than a locator."

"Get it out," I cried. "Just cut it out."

"It is your choice," he said, after sweeping me up in his arms and holding me tight. "On the other hand, if it begins not sending the correct data..."

I interrupted, "Yeah, yeah, I understand. KAG8 will know that I know." A shudder, and I whined, "Nohohoho." Where had it been so unsafe, so unprotected, that someone had the opportunity to insert a chip under my scalp, without me even having a clue? A memory of a memory niggled. Could those dreams that night in New Britain on Varga have been real?

Pearson set me upright and held me at arm's length, lending strength. He stated the obvious. "If you take it out, it may be replaced in ways you are unaware of."

After a heavy sigh, I gave him a dubious smile. Having him right in front of me was so...comforting...in spite of finding out about a computer chip under my scalp.

"You have changed," he stated. "Despite this," he pointed to the back of my head, "you are happy."

"Yes, even with this," I waved my hand in that direction, "life is better." And it was. I'd make my own demands of Pearson for honesty about the other women, eventually.

In the meantime, it took us a while to catch up on everything—in various manners. I didn't even allow Pearson to complete his sentence when he inquired if I wanted him to morph into Mac.

We started out tender, even tentative; elbows awkward, mouth missing mouth.

After falling onto the bed, I whispered, "I've missed you," and realized I had. No one else had ever been this tender with me, even Mac.

Pearson reached to hold me tight and rubbed his cheek on mine. Wrapping my arms around his neck, I kissed his closed eyes, his cheeks, his temples.

No longer caught up in an act meant to fill a void left by someone else long dead, my heart let go. Desire surged for the man—yes, the man—in my arms.

A small sob from me, and Pearson responded. He went in directions I didn't even know were possible. Tentative disappeared; replaced by hunger, urgency. We both rose to the occasion.

A good deal later, Pearson murmured in my ear, "I rectified KAG8's chart."

A chuckle escaped me; no one could say he wasn't good at multitasking. It took a moment to trace his path of logic, and he patiently waited. I shifted on the bed to be able to see him. The sheets were an incredibly expensive cotton from TohuMu. When I sat up, the top sheet slipped off.

"Oh, the Jyotish chart. You verified the start time?" This reminded me of the reason for meeting with Pearson. "Wait, that could help with the project I want to propose to you." I got serious. "I want to eradicate KAG8."

Pearson took my hands in his. "Great minds think alike," he said. "I have the exact moment for first turning on the computer that became KAG8, and have charted its trajectory through the centuries. With that information, we can strike at its weakest moments."

"That's it! I think maybe KAG8 is feeling some weakness. Maybe it's being pressured, forced into taking action, squeezed." A lovely fantasy of squeezing the computer flitted through my mind.

"I verified that it is in a bad astrological period." Pearson sat up slightly, and I shifted to accommodate. "While studying my own chart, I came across the writings of the Jyotish Master Irfan. For months, I tried to gain access to those writings—in vain, because the site was too protected. Finally permission was given, and after scanning most of the site I came across one reference indicating Irfan is alive."

Pearson excited about something was the same as a human: he was practically bouncing. "He is alive, and still working! In fact, I recently met with Master Irfan on Varga." Pearson's eyes widened in wonderment. "It appears the gentleman is cognizing the specific astrology for the newly settled planets."

"You went onto Varga? That's far too dangerous for you." Varga was one of the first planets to outlaw human-type robots.

Pearson dipped his head to acknowledge. "I consider the risk worthwhile if—when—KAG8 is destroyed."

"Are you working on this alone?"

"My people are trustworthy, but this project is crucial. To avoid KAG8 detecting even a hint of my intentions, I am careful to not disclose my plans."

We were silent, giving me time to catch up. "Has something changed? I don't remember you being as focused on this."

Even in the room with just the two of us, his whisper was barely audible. "I identified a marker for its connections, with which I have been tallying KAG8's human and robot agents, as well as locations including backups."

A thrill ran up my spine. "Let me help. As a wormhole pilot, I can go all over the place."

Pearson's lack of surprise about my new pilot status verified that he'd been keeping tabs on me.

"Congratulations on your commission, by the way." He leaned against the headboard, considering the possibilities. "If you want to help, you would need a reason for traveling. KAG8 is watching you, obviously."

"Yeah, I need to either get my shuttle cleaned of monitors or change ships." While considering the possibilities, I smoothed the sheets. "A job that goes lots of places would be good." The logic of the situation played out in my mind, "but I wouldn't be in control of my schedule." I blew out a breath. "And if you hired me, you-know-who would attack my family."

From his reaction, perhaps Pearson didn't know everything about my life.

"Remember the contact information for my father?" I asked. "We recently spent a little over a week together. Well, together with Dad— and his very large family." A slight eye roll escaped me. "Then KAG8 sent pirates to the planet, driving home the point that I am supposed to be out and about looking for SivSat."

"You are safe," said Pearson, while tucking a curl behind my ear. "Thus they wreaked minimal damage." At my grimace, he enveloped me in his arms. "I am sorry. Is there anything I can do for them?"

After a quick shake of the head from me, he said, "Perhaps we can prevail upon Newcastle to give you projects. He could provide you with a better ship and a protective crew."

"How is it you and Iain are cooperating? Didn't seem to be the case before. Are you certain he's safe?"

"One of his brothers was killed by pirates recently." After my moan of sympathy, Pearson said, "It has been difficult for the family. I pointed out to him we are resisting the entity in control of the pirates."

"I saw two men on Varga who looked enough like him to be his brothers. His family seems to be close."

"Yes, two brothers. Though now, only one. Thus, he wants to cooperate in every manner possible."

"By the way, Iain was invited to assist SivSat. By Trotaka." Pearson showed as much surprise as I'd felt. His face went blank, while his mental gears churned. "Actually, that makes sense."

"Really? How so."

Pearson seemed about to respond, but then he switched back to his project. "If I provide a method for searching for KAG8 nodes, you can transfer the information into the database."

"Nodes?"

"I have been collecting data for years, checking for markers in the data stream, to create a map of its agents and backups," he said softly. "Now, I control a KAG8 company for access to its computer facilities, with which I have become better at anticipating movements. Nevertheless, a strike at KAG8 has to be all at once or the computer will reboot, which is what happened when I tried to do this four hundred years ago."

"We'll figure out a way to do it out of nowhere, a total surprise," I said. "Like the way jaguars on my father's planet attack."

Pearson began whispering, and again I had to lean in.

"It was too easy for my broker to acquire the company. To the point that KAG8 probably cooperated. In other words, KAG8 may be ready to take action. We may be running out of time."

□□□

34 days remain before enforced self-destruction of KAG84950.301.

No self-destruct instructions detected for humanoid robot.

Chapter 21

As we strolled out to the suite's living room, I said, "You didn't seem surprised about me becoming a wormhole pilot."

He looked a little sheepish. "I located Edith Holmes-Fong within days of your departure. She mentioned enough for me to calculate your path and on which cruiser."

Into my mind sprang a memory of the brown-haired woman in Paris, taunting me about time spent with Pearson.

"You know, if you wanted to keep in touch with your harem, I wish you would have said something. How many other things are you not telling me?"

He sat, face blank, cogs whirling. "Why would you say that?"

"About not telling me? Isn't it obvious?"

"No, what you said about my...did you call it harem? I have seen none of those women since we were on the Earth space station before we went to India."

He appeared truly mystified. My own cogs began turning. A detail emerged from that afternoon in the hotel grand ballroom with Edith and the woman. There had been a certain coldness in the woman's eyes that was now terribly similar to interactions with KAG8. I moaned out loud.

Pearson said, "I am sorry I did not inform you of Mac's life."

With a quick breath, I stood up to pace, stopping only in front of a painting of deep space.

"Do you want the entire story?" asked Pearson.

"Why did you keep it from me?"

"He hoped I would make the difference to transport you home."

"What if I showed up in the middle of their marriage ceremony? Or better yet, when they were boinking and making the baby?"

He leaned his head to one side. "Rachel's notes indicated that she had to appear at the airport in a way that would minimize problems. Mac hoped that would be the case for you, too."

"And the fact I never did appear?"

"They divorced later, because he remained optimistic you would show up. And Rachel stopped wanting to help because the thought of not having their little girl was too painful."

Did I want to know what happened to Mac after that? No.

Pearson said, "The child grew up, and improved my design until she passed away at a very old age." He had one more shocker. "Rachel named her Donna."

I stared at him, open-mouthed. "You're kidding. Did Rachel remember Donny?"

"When I met Donny on the cruise from Adalans to Earth, I reviewed all my memories of Rachel. And identified none indicating that she specifically remembered him."

I rubbed my face, relieved those old emotions were no longer knocking me off my feet. "Again, why didn't you tell me?"

"If I told you, you would have given up on trying to go back."

And your programming couldn't allow that.

I said, "You seem to be okay with me knowing now."

"Now, we work on eradicating KAG8."

Another, different program, but programming nonetheless.

There was something about the entire drama that had never made total sense. "Do you understand why KAG8 is so intent on all this?"

"Perhaps KAG8 is driven by hard programming to capture SivSatyananda at any cost. Or the need for power over others."

"I never got a sense the Key Crystal bestowed power."

"Agreed," he said. "The Key is for locating the Crystal Ceres.

And, although Ceres is powerful, as in accomplishing a goal, it does not actually bestow power."

"How do you know that?"

"Before you arrived, I searched for the bigger crystal."

This was news to me. "Did you ever find it?"

"No, only rumors, false trails. Whoever is protecting it is good. On the other hand, I began to suspect I was coming across people who were connected to that crystal through time, an idea that was more useful to pursue."

"Through time?" I prompted.

"Incarnated over and over again."

"Reincarnation?" We'd spoken about it intellectually. Not with the idea of proof.

"I notice patterns," said Pearson. After a pause, he continued. "Reincarnation allows a soul to start over, which seemed to be the case for some of those people I recognized. Starting over provides an opportunity to do better the next time. Or to forget."

Unlike you, dear Pearson, with no chance of forgetting anything.

Identified and located: Male human with entire set of eleven DNA markers of Dr. Sterling Fahlsteder.

Name: Hainrich Fletcher.

Fletcher notified of his status as new incarnation of Dr. Sterling Fahlsteder.

Monitor attempts by Fletcher to locate KAG84950.301 and claim assets.

Anticipate and nullify efforts by Fletcher.

□□□

My robot friend reminded me it was less than an hour before my "carriage" would be picked up by a cart-bot.

"Show me the steps."

I had been taking notes on what would be my search parameters for KAG8 when Pearson abruptly whipped around to peer at the suite's door to the hallway. He jumped up and began pulling me toward the bedroom. Only then did I register the scratching outside in the corridor.

Next moment, the door thumped open, and Pearson propelled me in front of him into the next room.

"Give it up, robot," a man's voice growled. "Come with me now and we can avoid destroying this room." The smell of scorched metal from a laser burn warned me to avoid touching the doorjamb.

"It is a bounty hunter," Pearson whispered as he pushed me in back of him.

Another shot angled into our room.

"You have a laser gun?" I glanced over at where the shot had hit; no need to allow a fire to start.

Pearson moaned something about not being able to shoot unless protecting a human—and that I wasn't actually in danger.

"I can shoot," I said. Being attacked was getting to be irritating. "Where's your laser?"

Pearson only shook his head. "If I leave, the problem disappears."

Someone else joined the chaos in the other room, perhaps the floor manager. "Brandishing and using a laser weapon in this establishment is unacceptable," said a man, with what I'd come to recognize as an upper- crust spacer accent. "The police have been contacted. I order you to cease immediately."

"Who the hell are you?" replied the shooter. "This is none of your business. I am a lawful bounty hunter, deputized to return that robot to Varga. Get out of my way."

It sounded like the gentleman intended to make it his business. "This establishment does not care what mere planet deputized you. You must drop the weapon immediately."

The last I heard from Pearson was a low, "They will return for the laundry basket. I promise to contact you."

The hotel's agent was remarkably fast in corralling the bounty hunter. Clearly, the guy was scrambling to avoid his license being revoked due to all the threats from the hotel.

Since it was imperative that I not be noticed in Pearson's company, retreating to the laundry basket seemed the best course of action. True to Pearson's word, a few minutes later the door opened again and another cart-bot took control of my basket.

On the other end of the return trip to Newcastle's hotel, another door closed on darkness, and Iain flicked on the light before unpacking me from the laundry.

"How did everything go?" he asked with the kind of cheeriness indicating at least he'd gotten enough sleep. "My ship doesn't leave until late this afternoon and they will be loading until then. I'll probably stay here for the day. What about you?"

It was about five in the morning. I was whacked.

"My shuttle is docked not too far from here."

"Shuttle. Sounds spacious."

He didn't know the half of it.

Iain swept back his blond hair, which he must have professionally trimmed every week considering how it was always impeccable. "Pearson already messaged me, which is how I knew you would arrive soon." He brought out his pad and handed it over. "I admit to not understanding his plan, though I'm happy to run with it." After pointing to one part of the message, he said, "Pearson asked me to hire you, and send you throughout the galaxy. Even implying I might remain with you to guarantee your safety."

Being surprised only at how quickly it was all developing, I responded with a *what-can-I-say?* expression.

He said, "If this will defeat those bastards, I'm happy," and then tilted his head to the side. "Why doesn't Pearson simply point the authorities at this problem?"

Huh. Iain remained unaware of Pearson's actual nature. "Did he tell you who is behind the attacks?"

"He was vague about that."

With a bounty hunter already on Pearson's trail, I needed to not complicate things further.

"The way to fight this is through identifying hidden personnel, even robots. It—I mean, the boss—has slipped away before, so Pearson is being careful to avoid attracting too much attention."

My explanation must have satisfied him. Iain asked, "You have your wormhole pilot's license, correct?"

Probably Newcastle Industries would have a wormhole pilot on board who I could report to officially, and hopefully he didn't need to know my license would be up for review in a few months. "Yes."

"Good." He typed something on his pad and hit a button. "My assistant will find a vessel in need of a wormhole pilot. There's a silver lining in all this. We'll become good friends. And maybe I'll be able to convince you of the merits of a more pleasurable pace of life." A quick wiggle of his eyebrows, then he urged, "Relax. Enjoy." He looked around the room again and said, "I'm starving. Let's order breakfast."

Later in his living room, as we sat at the table loaded with breads and jams and even some eggs, Iain turned on the television and clicked to the news.

Varshana Vagwhatar was on the screen.

"And to complete our report..." The visual changed to a hotel door in a hallway that looked remarkably like the one I'd seen last night on our way to this room. "We wonder about the state of Lady Carlene Joelle Bravard of Varga, considering her fiancé Lord Iain Newcastle has been closeted all night with a common trollop. That, after parading the woman over the entirety of Ambient Space Station last evening." Varshana flashed a clear photo of me, walking beside Iain on our way into this hotel. "And that's it for now, from your InsideStory."

My appetite disappeared. Not Iain's. In fact, he reached for another slice of toast.

"You appear totally used to this kind of attention."

He sighed. "I become more concerned when the tabloids make things up." And shrugged one shoulder. "I learned a long time ago to simply lead my life. Worrying about people watching me will only hurt me, not them." He paused before taking a bite. "But I've never heard little Miss InsideStory avoid someone's name, like just now, and use such," he searched for the right word, "colorful language."

"Varshana Vagwhatar and I came across each other once. And it appears she blames me for losing something important to her."

As Iain continued with his breakfast, I had to grant he certainly knew how to keep things in perspective.

"Wait," I said. "You're engaged to be married. For her, doesn't this kind of scrutiny hurt?"

Iain set down his utensils and gazed at me squarely. "Now that we will be working together closely," he smiled at the prospect, "I should probably take the time to explain more of my life to you. May I?"

"If you'd like."

"I'd like," he said. "Carlene and I have known each other since we were children. Our fathers are alternately business partners and to-the- death competitors. It was decided we would marry when I was ten and she was four. We both like each other, and have no illusion about loving each other. In fact, Carlene is in love with a man she met on Earth right after she graduated from school."

The frankly stated facts were riveting.

"Another thing—the more I get into trouble, the less people will wonder where she is. And I care about her enough to cover for her even if I get a little scorched."

I had to know. "She is with..."

"Her lover. And if I know Carlene, she is trying to become pregnant so she can break our betrothal. I fear for her, however, if she does take that route."

❑❑❑

33 days before enforced self-destruction for KAG84950.301.

Chapter 22

Upon return to the shuttle, I broke the news to Nick and Lee. They both kind of got a glazed look at various points in the story. It was cute the way they'd glance at each other meaningfully.

Nick piped up. "Could we join the ship with Pearson, or at least one of the ships in his company?"

I was just happy KAG8 hadn't picked up on Pearson and me getting together. The bounty hunter had probably caught sight of me, though evidently the computer didn't control him.

"Probably, but I can't contact him directly. There needs to be no connection to me."

Later, Nick carried a note from me to Pearson, asking him to warn my father that the secret bunker was no longer safe for the family.

By the next morning, Iain had arranged for a couple of his employees to take the shuttle back to my father. Lee and Nick took off for Pearson's office, and I bundled Bill and my stuff over to my new ship.

At the spacecraft, Iain explained we would be traveling with a frigate delivering special-order parts; for our ship, he would be the pilot. "You'll get to show your brilliance by transiting us from one solar system to another."

I'd just secured my luggage in a tiny bedroom next door to Iain's. Two more doors led from the central hallway, to the kitchen/dining area and to the bridge. Metal walls were etched with flowers and vines. The "floor" was carpeted for the few times the craft would be in a gravity environment, though it was clear the carpet covered hatches to storage areas.

"There's no wormhole pilot?" I asked. "Who was here before?" Iain's face fell. "That man is on leave. His wife was on the ship with my brother, when the pirates destroyed it."

He looked so sad, I reached for his hand.

"Don't tell my family, but George was my favorite." Iain's eyes were turned toward me, but he wasn't looking at me. "We were barely a year apart. Hadrian is so much older and Penelope a good ten years younger."

It didn't take much to urge him on.

"It was the first voyage that George had captained in a long time. He much preferred life in Canterbury over space travel." Iain gazed down the hallway, his mind back somewhere in time with his brother.

"What is your happiest memory with him?"

Iain jerked a little at the question, but a grin quickly appeared. "Playing tricks on Hadrian. George was brilliant at coming up with new schemes, like the time... Well, maybe I won't give you the details on that one. Anyway, George would dream them up. I'd figure out how to execute, and then we'd both hide out, watching." Iain smiled, though his eyes still were pinched. "Anyway." He waved toward my room. "Get some rest. We start early tomorrow."

After Iain shut his door behind him, I floated there a bit, kind of wishing I'd had a sister or a brother. But then I realized that the man I'd seen in the communications office in New Britain—the one who had looked so much like Iain—was now dead. I felt sick to my stomach, and I didn't even know him. Maybe because my half-siblings had managed to entwine themselves in my heart, even after just a week.

The next morning, Iain remained pensive while he worked with the frigate to get us underway. He didn't bring up the subject again, though I detected an edge of rather-determined optimism when he teased me at dinner a couple of evenings later.

"Alexa, this next station has a unique 'amusement park.' Full-body immersion. You game?"

"You mean like whooshing down," my arms shot out in front of me, "into a pool of water?"

Judging by his momentary blank look, he'd never had that pleasure. "Perhaps," he acknowledged. "Mostly this is... delightfully sensual." The way he emphasized that last word left little to the imagination.

Seemed to me that he might simply be trying to distract himself. Whatever the case, it was clear that Iain Newcastle would be a dangerous traveling companion. "I think I need to focus on the project." When I had stumbled onto a storage area on our ship, I'd realized the sheer variety of his leisure pursuits. "And should probably get started right away."

Iain shrugged in resignation and trailed after me to the tiny cubicle set aside as my office. Bill was there. A few moments passed while Iain checked out the area, pondering Bill.

"Your dog is unique."

No way around it. Sooner or later, he would know. I should offer an explanation, with as little detail as possible.

"Bill is robotic." At his name, my dog looked over at me and then at Iain.

"Amazing." Iain's eyebrows slowly rose. "And expensive."

"He was a gift."

Obviously, Iain wondered from whom, and the possibilities behind such remarkable technology. The screen in front of me was a perfect excuse to not look his way. He must have gotten the hint because he soon left us, saying, "I'll get you that schedule you requested."

□□□

Humanoid robot and human female communicated: deliver retribution.

Compulsory self-destruction in 32 days.

❑❑❑

As we powered from one solar system to another over the first week, it turned out that Pearson's techniques for following and capturing data- nodes were not difficult, just time consuming. At two space stations and one planet, I slogged away at the details. Hopefully, the accumulation of data meant we were drawing the noose on KAG8's safe places.

A few days later, on the space station above a planet where Iain had gone to deliver several parts, I went in search of a shortcut between our docking space and the food court. The chef on board the frigate was too good—I needed less fattening food. After a nice dinner of salad and soup, I headed back to our craft to pick up Bill for a walk on the station. Bill had mentioned he wanted to warn me about something in my chart.

In the next-to-last corridor before the docking area, a door about twenty feet in front of me slammed open and music blared. Sounded like a bar. The door opened again, and out of the bar stumbled a man, then another, and another. They laughed and turned my direction.

Kick to the gut! One of them was that chief bandit from the attack on Uxmal, Dogo.

I did an about-face and headed back toward the food court, only about a hundred feet away but around a corner and a short hallway. Too quickly the smallest guy in the pack passed on my left, another on my right. When Dogo appeared in front of me, I stopped, hoping to avoid giving him the opportunity to make a grab.

Dogo crossed his arms and checked out certain parts of my anatomy. "Hello, Red. Miss me?"

A man loomed behind. I tried to sound tough, and failed miserably.

"If you come any closer I'll scream 'pirates.'"

Dogo threw out his hands. "Here to bring in the faithful, Red."

"Faithful—as in whatever that 'priest' comes up with next. Which is mostly death and destruction." I almost mentioned something about what they did to women, but decided to not introduce that concept at the moment.

"Now, now, this is just a friendly get-together, Red. Though we can arrange another chance for you to join the 'devotions.' If you beg real nice." His buddies snickered. "I notice you listened to the warning, though. Or maybe you've been looking for me?"

If I could hold them off long enough, someone might pass nearby. "None of the above."

Dogo took a step forward; the others slunk away. It no longer seemed to be Dogo. Unfortunately, something overly familiar to me instead. When the man spoke again, no humanity warmed the tone or content.

"I grow impatient." When I didn't respond, the menacing voice continued. "By not locating the desired human, you risk lives. One mother and child on Uxmal have paid the price. How many more are you willing to lose?"

No news had made it to me about a problem with Dad's family.

"When? How?" From the look of triumph on his face, I could only hope it wasn't little Itza and her mother. I wailed, "No! Why would you do that?"

"Failure to deliver results always produces consequences."

"How am I supposed to find SivSatyananda, if you can't?"

KAG8's stare through the pirate's eyes made it impossible to put one thought after another.

"The alternative is to use you as bait, to provoke the arrival of the desired human. Do you trust him to come to your rescue?"

SivSat had many more responsibilities in the galaxy than saving me, and I could accept that. On the other hand, I had to do something to protect the children. But what?

"I am looking for him. He is very difficult to locate if he doesn't want to be found." I pleaded, "I'll look harder."

KAG8 brought up a threat tailored to my worst nightmare. "Your lack of imagination only serves to offer temptation to my soldiers. Locate SivSatyananda, or they will know you thoroughly. Otherwise, reminders will be delivered via your family."

The tension, as in my heart trying to escape through my throat, was broken by the sound of heels beating a path down the corridor. A woman with short, shocking purple hair came around the corner and strode at us.

She stopped beside me and turned to glare at the man. I gaped at her. Once I got past the purple hair, I almost blurted out a demand about how it was that Edith Holmes-Fong was standing beside me, looking like she could take on just about anybody.

The woman and KAG8 bristled at each other.

Could she have actually intimidated the computer, or did it decide that enough had been said? Whatever the case, KAG8 abruptly vanished and once more Dogo was present in front of us.

Dogo also attempted to establish his male dominance by sneering at the woman. He said nothing before turning to leave—until he reached the corner, where he glanced back and pointedly looked at me. "Remember, babe, you're mine."

The other goons followed him. After the little guy was out of sight, the woman and I gaped at the empty space in front of us.

"Are you all right?" asked the woman, who in front of my eyes morphed from butch-tough to the epitome of motherly concern. "Who are those men?"

Still vibrating at the visuals prompted by KAG8's threat, all I could manage was, "Bastards."

She cocked her eyebrow, expecting more. When I said nothing, she asked, "Are you Alexa Jane Alden?"

Admit to my identity, or run? I was no longer certain. "Who are you? And why do you look so much like someone I know?"

The woman made another instant chameleon change, to guarded. "At the moment that would be irrelevant. Are you Alexa Jane Alden?"

I responded with, "No answers until you tell me who you are."

"My name is Marion Bahar."

So, not Edith. "That's a start, but I still don't know who you are."

"I am a trusted advisor to a certain countess, the mother of a young woman you've been seen with."

Penelope? But she's no countess. Perhaps Penelope's mother?

The bar's door blasted open again, and two more drunken men wobbled out. Marion cut her eyes in that direction and then back at me. "Let's walk to somewhere safer."

I couldn't agree more, so followed along in the direction of the food court I'd just left. Amazing how just a couple of corners could change the environment, because soon we were strolling among mothers and their children.

I asked, "Why are you looking for m...for Alexa Jane Alden?"

Marion brought out a pad, paged to a video and handed it over. "This young woman certainly appears to be you, and you'll notice she's standing beside Lady Carlene Bravard."

The image was Uxmal, when several of my young half-sisters had been singing at an event set up by Nish to lift spirits after the attack. The littlest singer, Itza, the one who always climbed onto my lap, had stolen the show by doing an impromptu dance. I didn't think long about Itza.

The woman standing beside me in the image was Lee, not Carlene.

"Please," said Marion, "Carlene's mother is desperate to locate her."

My mind was whirling faster than little Itza, may she remain forever safe.

Marion continued pleading her case. "Carlene's fiancé maintains no knowledge of her location. But here she is, with you, and you are working for Iain Newcastle." With those compelling eyes, she willed me to spill the space dust.

Having no clue of what would hurt either Iain or Lee, I remained silent.

The woman tried again. "If her father locates Carlene before her mother, the consequences will be dire. Please, tell me where I can find Carlene."

I had to ask. "Do you know Edith Holmes-Fong?"

This seemed to catch the woman by surprise. She didn't immediately respond.

"You could be her twin sister. Except for, well, the purple hair."

Marion's face softened momentarily, but then hardened. "Edith and I do not communicate. If you speak to her, do not feel compelled to inform her of my whereabouts." She practically took my shoulders to shake them. "Could you please help me locate Carlene?"

"I'm sorry, I can't tell you what I don't know." Not really a lie. Technically, I didn't know for certain whether Lee and Nick had joined Pearson's ships. And I couldn't know for certain Lee's wishes. Marion Bahar wanting to avoid her family was no different from what Lee was obviously doing. "Nevertheless, if possible, I will do my best to forward a message."

Marion Bahar pursed her lips, perhaps realizing she'd gotten as much as possible at the moment. As she reached into the heavy leather pouch around her middle, she said, "Carlene needs to speak with her mother soon. Very soon. Here is my card." She cocked her head. "And, besides Carlene, I'm worried about you. Those were dangerous men. Be careful, okay?" With that, she strode away.

Emotions about Lee—or Carlene—and Iain stormed through my head. I liked both of them. Trusted both of them, to a certain extent. That I'd come across Iain's misplaced betrothed—no matter that they were not really attached to each other—was astonishing.

Collapsing into a chair at a big table with lots of people, another issue bubbled up in my brain. How did Dogo know where to find me? The answer popped up and I hit my head with my hand. "Duh, the locator chip."

Chapter 23

Iain and I were at lunch in the frigate's dining room; I preferred meals on the frigate because it had gravity.

The space station was visible through the thick window beside us. Music played in the background, almost romantic. Iain's doing, not mine. *Perhaps what he does when a female is around.*

Iain's response to news of Marion Bahar searching for Carlene, or Lee, had been rather underwhelming.

"Carlene was on Uxmal? Forgive me, but from what I've heard about the planet it doesn't sound to be her kind of place at all."

My real concern was her family. "Is she in trouble with her parents?"

"Carlene's father is someone to be reckoned with. On the other hand, her mother always feels the need for guidance. Thus, it may simply be due to the influence of that woman." Iain cocked his head and cut his eyes at me in curiosity. "What do you think of this Nicholas character?"

To Iain's credit, he was more troubled about my interlude with Dogo. From then on, he insisted on going with me everywhere— a situation that made any further covert investigation impossible because people always recognized him, especially women. It was a little irritating.

On the next space station, which happened to be near TohuMu, Iain and I were strolling through the shopping section when a woman squealed, "Iain Newcastle," and pushed in between us. I swear he flinched. While tossing her long bottle-blonde hair, she cooed "dearest," then took his arm and steered him away.

Deciding to salvage at least some dignity, I gazed into the window in front of me—full of little pyramids about the size of ring boxes. The boxes took turns beaming up holograms, some as tall as four feet, mostly of family scenes. Each tableau had the feel of staged family pictures in front of fake backdrops. I got the sense that what was on sale wasn't the cool technology, but the service of producing them.

When Iain returned five minutes later, he picked up our conversation as if nothing had happened.

Such annoyances aside, Iain's presence did provide extra safety. Dogo and company were nowhere around. Still, the problem of transferring data to Pearson remained. Wherever I went, com-lines were tapped, and Iain was getting offended. One afternoon, he poked his head into my cubicle. "All messages from us are now blocked, which should be impossible. Our communications should be more protected than those of military installations."

Glancing over from the screen in front of me, I said, "You can't do anything about it. KAG8 is relentless."

Iain responded like my father.

"Am I hearing you correctly? Several times now, you've said KAG8." He meticulously pronounced it as kag-ate. "Some kind of code?"

How much to tell him? "Pearson calls it that."

He glanced at me sideways. "It?"

My father had agreed to say nothing about Pearson to anyone. More people—including Iain—knowing the entirety of Pearson's situation would be worrisome. I bit the inside of my lip.

"A computer," I stressed the word, "is the source of all this trouble, one that definitely does not follow any programming regarding the protection of humans."

"Related to the pirates?" And thus to his brother's death. Behind the bravado, Iain cared about his family.

"Yes."

"And this effort is to neutralize the computer, and thus the pirates?" he asked.

I nodded.

"And you are involved in this because?"

My smile was wry. "Remember the little crystal you and your family wanted from me?" Iain made a moue of distaste as I said, "Well, KAG8 also wanted it."

His face crumpled at the complications. He'd no idea. Then it appeared that a part of the puzzle came together for him. "Then, maybe this 'it' is what the family legend was referring to. The story always sounded ludicrous to me, but a computer could explain much." He gazed at the data on my screen for a moment before saying, "What fool would create something like that to last so long?"

"Someone who wanted the crystal as much as—or more than—your family," I said.

Iain got a pained look on his face. "Did the crystal end up under its control?"

"No. SivSatyananda has it."

"The same wise man who was looking for me?"

Watching Iain try to fit all the pieces together almost made me laugh.

He held up one hand before saying, "And Pearson thinks he can defeat this thing with data?"

"Pearson's been working on this algorithm for a long time"—a really long time—"and knows how to use it."

Finally, Iain smiled. "Okay, then, off we go on the hunt for data." He seemed to make a resolve. "However, as soon as possible I'm arranging for some fun. You might get worry lines if you keep up this pace forever."

Fun. At one point in my life, fun had been easy. The norm.

But I hadn't even thought about it since arriving in this century. KAG8 seemed to have a genius for showing up the moment I began to relax. The only remedy for the situation? Get rid of KAG8.

"I need to transfer this data to Pearson. Maybe I should check with him."

A strange look crossed Iain's face and he tapped the door frame for a moment before floating away. Did I hear him whisper, "tryst?" Nevertheless, he arranged another meeting. Evidently, the secret ins and outs of space-station hotels were a big part of all those "fun" things he knew so much about.

A few days later in another hotel suite, I made my pitch to Pearson. "I mean it, a communications chip is the best way."

He responded as if I needed the process explained in detail.

"Actually, it is not a chip like you are familiar with, but more of a filament—organic. Even with that, it is more intrusive than a simple locator, which is just under your scalp. It is in your brain."

I closed my eyes. We were sitting in the living room of the suite, having avoided the bed—mostly Pearson's doing, though I hadn't protested. I'd been dealing with the prospect of someone messing with my skull, which made my stomach churn.

"Could it work? The data could be transferred that way?"

"You would have to physically read it to me."

Hours. Every day. "What if it was possible for you to see through my eyes? I'd just need to view the screen, right?"

"That requires an even more intrusive technology, to connect with both the visual and auditory cortexes."

The plan had seemed simple the night before. *Did it suddenly get cold in here?* I rubbed my arms.

"It's not as invasive as the chip that KAG8 uses, right? Not to the point of being able to take over my body's movements?"

"No," he admitted.

My face in my hands, I said, "It's the only method not likely to be traced." Pearson gazed at me with such compassion. "I collect truly helpful information every day, but I can't get it to you, and we can't depend on this ruse working all the time."

Again he tried to talk me out of it. "I have heard of cases where such technology was suborned."

Rocking back and forth, I wrapped my arms around myself. *Be brave.* No better way to fight KAG8.

"Less likely if you're involved," I replied. "And if anyone can come up with protections, it's you. I can't see any other way to get the data to you fast enough."

One part of me speculated on whether I'd lost my mind, while another part had complete confidence in Pearson's ability to keep me safe. Even another part of me marveled at how I'd slid right back into our relationship.

Despite that last thought, because Pearson continued resisting I pointed out the fact that would make it inevitable. "You said KAG8 seems ready to take action."

That afternoon, we checked me into a high-tech spa, officially for cosmetic surgery.

To hire a neurosurgeon, Pearson tapped one of the hospitals he'd funded decades earlier. The surgeon insisted on working in his own space, thus I had to be moved anonymously. Not all robots were compromised by KAG8, though it would be foolhardy to take chances. Therefore, we resorted to the low-tech trick of leaving a line of pillows under a blanket on my bed. Pearson paid the spa for the extra steps.

The surgeon explained that, although the practice remained highly unusual because of the cost, he himself used the technology to assist with surgeries. The filament we were considering was not the most complex. Even so, it would take a week after insertion for basic connections within my brain in the auditory area to develop. About two weeks later, links to visual impulses on their way to the back of the brain would begin working. The operation consisted of a micro incision at the top of my skull and required the same recovery time as a major cosmetic procedure.

Both of us reminded the doctor to take out the chip under my scalp and hand it over to Pearson. I'd determined to wear that particular bit of KAG8 interference in a ring or something. Visions of frustrating KAG8 danced in my head as I slipped under anesthesia in the surgery room.

Must commend technology, it was surprising how easily the surgery went. By the next morning I was walking around, smelling the flowers Pearson had delivered.

And as far as Iain knew, I had simply spent the night with Pearson.

Unfortunately, KAG8 must have found out about Pearson and me, because a message arrived later that same morning.

Dearest, the palace is destroyed and my people have fled the cities. That "it" of yours evidently does not know how to keep a bargain.

Also, my heart is broken because, without warning a few days ago, Raxka and her daughter Yudelle died. We are still trying to understand what happened. I've wondered if there could be a connection to "it," but can't tell one way or another.

Murdoch Callaghan is sending a ship for us. You will be able to reach us on Adalans soon. I love you. Be very careful. **Dad**

Chapter 24

"You allowed them to put something like that in your brain?" yelled Iain, outraged. "So—what?—you're reporting to a computer somewhere, or something?"

I was just relieved he had provided a plausible cover story. Something told me not to mention that it was Pearson I'd be reporting to. "It's the only way to transfer the data without going back and forth in a laundry basket."

"And what happens when this KAG8 identifies a way to take over the thing in your brain? Will you begin having a relationship with it, too?" He stopped pacing and glared at me, hands on hips.

I blinked a couple of times. "Pearson was concerned about the same possibility, so he included extra precautions—"

"Kind of Pearson to handle that detail for you."

"Which is what Pearson does." I don't think any part of my tone implied Iain didn't handle things for me or that Pearson was better than him. I mean, it had actually been Pearson's job to take care of me. It wasn't Iain's job, and he certainly had plenty of other females in line for that kind of attention.

Iain must have decided he heard something in my voice, though.

"Ah, yes. Perfection incarnate." Iain glanced at the ring I wore on my right hand. Again.

In perfect timing my phone chimed, indicating a call from Pearson. For short communications, he'd set up several fictitious accounts. Iain's face went blank, except for his jaw, which throbbed.

I ignored the call. "All of this is to accomplish something much more important than me."

"I suppose it was Pearson's idea?"

"No, mine."

He stood there, nodding, not believing me. "Better answer that call."

❑❑❑

19 days before KAG84950.301 self-destruction.

❑❑❑

Despite the extra effort involved because of life around Iain, his family's connections were more than a little useful. One of the nifty options available to those ship owners with the right relationships and the ability to pay the steep price was plugging into surveillance systems on various stations. The service made it possible for me to physically check data-nodes. Sometimes addresses pointed to robots, other times an office. A few pointed to humans.

With all the data I'd collected in the previous week, though, something nagged at me. Of course I double-checked, because surely Pearson's algorithm couldn't be wrong. Nevertheless, it simply felt wrong for KAG8 lynchpins to be a diaper service, a blue cart-bot delivering food at a kitchen court, and a mild-mannered preacher. I turned to Iain.

"Would you mind reviewing this data?" Without specifying my concerns, I pointed to the screen.

Before turning his attention to my data, he closed a message on his pad while shaking his head. He didn't bother to share what seemed to annoy him.

"Names, numbers. Are those addresses?" When I nodded, he scanned again. "Looks good to me."

He'd drawn close to me, arm leaning almost around my

shoulder, half friend/half flirt. That it had become common almost felt good. Nevertheless, my instinct warned that it would be best if I ignored that last fact.

"How about now?" I asked.

With visuals added to some of the addresses, about halfway down the list he asked, "Is that a church?" When I said yes, he continued, "And this is for our project? Huh. I've certainly come across clergy whose calling did not completely benefit their parishioners, but this is extreme."

"How long will we stay at this station?"

"We could leave this evening," he said.

I said, "Back soon."

When he asked where I was going, as if I couldn't be trusted, I called out, "In time. Promise."

Paper products being hard to come across in space, diapers had long ago made it full circle back to cloth. The diaper service was in an office zone of the station and the door had a screen with a video of laughing babies on it. I pushed through, into the world of parenthood. Not only was the place a diaper service but also a busy daycare center. A mother with an infant and a two-year-old squeezed past me on her way out, soon followed by the arrival of a father, identified by the welcoming squeal of his son.

Outside the door I searched up and down the corridor. The only business possibly out of place was a smoke shop across the hallway. That people still used tobacco was mind-boggling to me. I mean, it was a space station with limited supply of air. At least the shop wasn't thriving.

A quarter hour later, I stood in line at the kitchen court where the blue cart-bot worked. It delivered food and bussed tables, sometimes efficiently sometimes not. If it was being a secret agent spy, the children it mostly served weren't helping its task.

Next data point: the church. The entrance was along a blank wall, barren of even the huge news screens. Around the door was a fake small white steeple; perhaps Methodist. Two women walked out, allowing me the opportunity to slip inside. Yep. Methodist. If something unusual was going on in there, they were good at hiding it.

With indications that at least three data-nodes were wrong, I headed back to the ship, heart heavy. Iain was readying our shuttle to follow the frigate, so I left him alone and went directly to my little office.

Pearson's reflection in the screen in front of him came into focus in my mind, allowing me to see him through his eyes. I hadn't expected to be able to see through Pearson's eyes, but was happy that turned out to be the case. After responding to my hello, he pushed a button to save data and sat back. His grin took on a decided wolfish flair.

"I identified the base signature of KAG8's processing paths."

I swear he almost came close to hooting. Too bad I was about to deliver potentially catastrophic news. "Pearson, I'm almost certain at least some of the addresses are incorrect. Random physical addresses I just checked make no sense."

He protested, "We have only three solar systems to complete the original tally."

On the screen in front of him, Pearson mapped in the data from me. KAG8's nexus had expanded to almost double from just the month before. No possible way to accomplish our goal if all the sites were fully functional.

"Is there some way to spot-check the addresses?" I asked.

"The same method originally used to verify validity."

As I watched, he brought up a program and started it. Data zipped past on the screen. On the side, a metric showed green and red. Alas, more red than green—much more red.

"KAG8 may have begun scrambling the addresses of its backups." Backups. As in replicators? The size of the project went supernova. "Um, you have backups, too, right?"

He looked at the screen, which reflected back into his eyes and thus mine, and smiled—one of those smiles that had turned my knees to rubber in the past. But not this time, interestingly.

A screen to the right of Pearson began showing coding. I think he was working directly within the computer.

"Ajay, could you check more of the physical addresses? Any clean data you can amass will assist in breaking the modification algorithm."

I went looking for Iain.

We came to an agreement to keep our ship at the current position another day, while I mapped out the physical nodes. Iain offered to split the list with me, but before we headed out to check the nodes he made me promise I wouldn't go into any more dangerous zones. He relented only after I assured him I'd stay in populated areas. Even with that, I was forced to point out that Bill would be with me.

After a couple of hours of walking from point to point on the station, my dog commented, "We're taking a long walk today."

A man passing by us almost tripped over his feet when he realized the voice came from the direction of the floor. People traveled through space with their animals all the time, something made obvious during my trip from Adalans to Earth months ago. Inhabitants on space stations generally didn't keep large dogs, though I suspected the occasional bunny or hamster or cat lived behind closed doors.

"I'm about finished with my list."

Pearson might be happy with my findings. Out of seventeen

locations, even I had begun to recognize a pattern between improbable data-nodes and more logical KAG8 representatives. An obvious positive node was a politician who many considered to have received illegal payments from a large air-cleaning company. Another was a teller-bot for a bank. Not my bank, thank goodness, though I began considering methods for protecting my finances from snooping eyes.

If the last data point on my list was obvious one way or another, we might have the basis of a trend for Pearson.

After pushing through a couple of doors, I stood at the entrance to a deserted hallway. The last data-node appeared to be somewhere behind the tightly closed garage door thirty-five feet away at the end of a corridor. The hallway between the huge door and me was littered with low-slung containers about as tall as Bill. They were full of some kind of metal bits the size of marbles.

Not only did the door appear seriously locked, I was about as inconspicuous as a pink Band-Aid on an asteroid miner. A dirty yellow robot and a green one zipped by, one after the other. A mauve one—or dusty rose with all the soot—dragged over a pallet with old robot parts: torsos, legs, arms. The heads weren't too lifelike, thank goodness.

Soon after the bots left, a low whine came from behind the door.

It quickly ramped up high enough to make any biological dog start howling. Then a small explosion sounded. All this happened within ten seconds. About a minute later, the door jerked and began to roll up from the bottom. I scurried behind one of three pallets piled with big chunks of scrap metal and hunkered down, holding Bill. As I watched, another low container appeared— maybe pushed out by someone, or something—and the door slammed shut. About two minutes later, the whine started up again.

Later, after two more containers of metal chunks were pushed out, the door opened higher than usual and a tiny tugboat robot emerged, aiming at me. This wasn't a restricted area. Still, I sweated.

The tug-bot didn't notice me. Instead, it stopped at the first pallet, piled with the defunct robots. It latched onto the pallet and headed back toward the overhead door, which remained open barely enough to accommodate the pallet. The bot pushed aside containers of metal nuggets as it powered through.

Pearson contacted me via our mental link. His presence was in my head before his thought.

"Ajay, how are you doing on the locations?"

"I'm at the last place on my list. And I have some good data for you." "Testing the algorithms should begin soon. Returning to the ship would be helpful."

"I don't know," I said. "This place is a challenge because of a locked door. But leaving here seems a shame, since I'm so close to having a full set of data. I wish there was a window on the door or something. Most of the nodes on my list have been easy to verify one way or another, by simply seeing them."

The door raised up again, one of those short containers emerged, and the door dropped back down. Something in me wasn't willing to give up.

"Pearson, you can talk with Bill, right?"

Bill looked up at me a split second later, and Pearson said, "Yes." "Can you see through his eyes and hear, too?"

Bill looked at my feet. Pearson said, "You are wearing turquoise boots."

I smiled. "I wonder if Bill could scoot into the area and watch and listen for just a little bit. What do you think?"

Bill said, "That is a better idea than you going in."

I asked Pearson, "You promise to keep Bill on the side? No heroics?"

Pearson said he would, so I almost calmly watched my pooch slink toward the overhead door. He crouched in the corner behind a container of metal marbles. The next time the door rose, Bill snuck inside while another container was pushed out.

I should have asked to see through Pearson's eyes during the process, but I didn't want to interfere and cause a problem. It felt like a whole week passed with no word.

My heart jumped when from behind the door came a screech— a cross between an enraged gorilla and the ear-splitting shriek of a New York City subway on a really tight curve. Then the sound of a caveman trying to smash a creepy crawly. Another screech and I was at the door, searching on all sides for an override.

Bam-Bam kept at it, while I hit every button available.

At last, the door began to slide up and I dropped to the ground. With barely enough sense of self-preservation to look before rolling in, I glimpsed a humanoid robot wielding a steel beam at Bill.

Motherhood blossomed.

Under the door and back on my feet in the room, I grabbed a defunct leg from a heap nearby and ran at the bot, screaming. Its next hit would have connected with Bill. Fortunately, I distracted the robot and it missed.

The robot turned to square off with me. That it didn't immediately back off from a human instructing it to stop, and indeed began menacing me, told some rational part of my mind I'd located a true KAG8 data-node. No robot was supposed to ever endanger a human.

A whiff of something bitter and caustic drifted by my nose, maybe from the room behind Bill, who'd begun yapping like a Chihuahua.

I almost felt Pearson in my head, though he knew to not interrupt and was probably watching the whole thing from Bill's perspective. In fact, Bill began throwing himself at the back of the bot's legs and then running toward the little room.

I swung the metal leg. "Stop! Desist! Halt! Shut down!"

Human commands seemed to war with the bot's programming; it lurched in my direction, then fell back and let the metal bar drop. Again, it pitched itself toward me; and retreated, almost into passivity. Finally, it seemed to give up, simply standing in front of the door. Bill was behind the bot, so I moved forward to call for him.

Must have gotten too close, because the robot again raised its weapon.

Swinging the leg in my hands, I connected with the bot's metal bar with a ringing clank, my arms vibrating with a *bwang*.

Thank goodness for movies, because at least I had an idea to switch direction to match each new blow from the robot.

My shoulders tired quickly.

Tough.

The whole time, Bill was jumping at the back of the bot's knees, hitting them as hard as he could.

Despite the robot's superior strength, maybe because I continued to yell commands to stop, finally the bot fell backwards into the room after I landed a good blow.

Bill scooted out the door. I slammed it.

One of the bot's feet jammed the door open, however. The robot took advantage of the opening and grabbed at the edge of the door, crushing my fingers. I screamed in pain, probably also terror.

Even though the bot's hands would almost surely block my efforts to shut the door, I leaned against it. A little movement toward closed, but not enough, and the bot seemed to sense my intent. Its own struggle to get up intensified. I threw myself against the door, once, twice, a quick third time. And *finally!* a click said the door closed; one metal hand and some fingers lay where they dropped. I don't think they were moving.

The bot was up and pounding on the door from the inside with its stumps almost immediately. Then I noticed the control panel. A big button called out to me. I slammed my fist on it.

The whine began low, and ratcheted up high. The robot kept pounding. *Thump. Thump. Thump.*

The explosion was deafening, that close. A sound of buckshot from inside the enclosure made me duck. When I finally opened the door, all that remained were a thousand metal marbles on the floor.

Hope the bot didn't have time to contact KAG8.

❑❑❑

Human female attempting to track KAG84950.301.

Response: Deliver data to piloting instructor.

Time: 12 days before self-destruction.

Chapter 25

Iain turned out to be way too adroit in extracting information about the battle with the robot, though probably my torn clothes and bruised hand had tipped him off the most. Alas, during Iain's grilling, I was so tired that I must have given more information than I intended on how intimately Pearson and I connected via the mind-chip. From then on, Iain became rather sensitive about me suddenly switching my attention inward.

I kept all that drama away from Pearson, however, since he was hard at work concocting an algorithm to counter KAG8's algorithm. He'd increased his computational capability to triple check all the old data.

And I became more adept at identifying KAG8 nodes, accumulating so much information that it was a challenge to simply move it past my eyes for Pearson to pick up.

"Exhausted," I announced to Iain. I'd been staring at a screen for hours. "Need a walk, and a nap." In truth, I could have happily laid my head down for a couple of days. Nevertheless, we were scheduled to leave the station in a little over an hour and if I wanted any exercise other than playing tug of war in free fall, I had to get it then.

"I'll go with you," said Iain. After that run-in with the robot, he'd been tagging along with me everywhere. Problem was, everyone made a big deal over him, to the point that it was impossible to enjoy a stroll.

I cut my eyes at him. "If you don't mind, a simple walk would be really nice—one without all the female attention. I'm even leaving Bill behind."

"I don't know."

He sounded as if it might break a rule or something, and it's possible I lost my temper a bit. I was really tired.

"Did I miss something, and somewhere along the way you became my parent?"

"When a person continually seeks out life-threatening situations, questions about their judgment arise."

"Excuse me, but no one appointed you my guardian. I can take care of myself just fine." I pushed off toward the portal to the float tube that would take me to the station. He moved as if to follow. "Don't even think about it."

In the station and walking briskly, it took not much time for me to calm down and realize that last statement had been rather unsmart. Technically, Iain was my boss, him being the captain of the vessel. He didn't have to bankroll this venture. This wasn't his drama. My little snit might endanger the goal of getting rid of KAG8, something far more important than the recent silliness.

Therefore, when I noticed Iain in the large common area near our dock, I didn't run in the other direction. Instead, I walked up and took my place beside him. Iain wore a hat and had made the effort to disguise his appearance a bit, so for once there weren't a dozen ladies around him vying for attention.

He smiled at me briefly before craning to see around a column. I noticed what he'd noticed: two open chairs. As soon as he began moving in that direction, though, a lady dropped into one of the chairs. He stopped and stepped back, seeming content to stand beside me. Anyway, the plastic-type chairs looked uncomfortable. Most everyone, instead, milled around in the group behind the seating. Iain's attention was on the stage, so I turned from studying the people to follow his gaze. A man sat on stage, holding an acoustic guitar.

"Wow," I said, "people still play those. I love that sound."

"Shhhh, they're about to begin."

The light went dusky, and a spotlight illuminated the man's hands on an intricately etched rosewood guitar.

One dulcet note, and another, then lilting tones began skipping up and down my spine. My, the man's fingers tripped the light fantastic. Drums drove the beat. No one kept still. Heads bobbed. Feet tapped. Delicate riffs followed by a blast-out-loud ditty, then swaying melodies, swept everyone along. People around us dancing, Iain turned and scooped me into his arms, twirling through the boisterous last curtain call. The crowd roared in rapture. Iain's laughing eyes gazed into mine, mirroring my own wild giggles.

This must have been what Pearson saw when he checked in on me. "Oh, sorry," sounded in my mind. Then blankness.

Mentally, I called out to him. "Pearson, are you there?" He wasn't. Iain jerked back. His expression went hard, guarded. Lips pursed, he scanned the crowd. I must not be as good as I hoped at carrying on a dual conversation.

From the zone, to all alone, in an instant.

□□□

9 days before enforced self-destruction.

□□□

Number two of the last three solar systems on our list to double check was on the other side of the wormhole in front of us. We were deep in the night cycle, with all other humans on the ship asleep, including Iain—who had barely spoken to me in days. I checked the pilot's database and leaned into the transit.

Waiting for me in that jump was a delightful surprise. As we came out the other side, something wondrous caught my attention. A thread of data about SivSatyananda, including a sense of light and power, golden. Never had I come across this at any other portal. Could SivSat have passed through? To where? Adalans lay two systems further along. Perhaps the many types of crystals on Adalans were as useful to him as they were to all the other planetary organizations. I shared the information with Pearson, but briefly. Although the scanner continued to show Iain's ship to be clear of monitors, I didn't want to take any chances.

Iain and I covered the system over several days. The three small space stations were easy, while an industrial planet with no breathable atmosphere and plenty of metals turned out to be more challenging. If anything, KAG8 was thorough. Similar to other systems, every outpost had at least twenty data-nodes, often more.

After delivering the goods to Pearson, I turned to the task of convincing Iain to go to Adalans. Someone in his home office had been increasingly adamant about him touching base soon. With each new message, Iain practically growled.

Strained relations with his family—which I gathered from his periodic mutterings about Hadrian—worked in my favor. I mean, in comparison with Hadrian, I was a cupcake. Still, it had taken some doing to get us to a friendly place again.

Then there was the issue of SivSatyananda, for which I laid on even more charm.

"You want to track SivSatyananda?" he demanded, surprised. "The same guru the Trotaka man mentioned?" When I nodded, Iain asked, "Why Adalans?"

I needed to back up a bit. "You know I meditate, right?"

He cocked his head in acknowledgement. "You mean, your habit of sleeping while sitting up?"

Maybe I'd been over-working and under-sleeping.

"Ah, you've noticed. There are times when I don't always fall asleep while meditating. And those times may be the reason I...am able to...pick up information while transiting through wormholes." When his eyes screwed in disbelief, I hurriedly said, "At least, that's my theory about why it happens."

"Never heard of anything like it."

"I've verified accuracy. Many times."

Iain turned to the pilot screen and brought up routes, wormholes, and transit time to Adalans, versus the company's headquarters. The news was not good. He asked, "Can it wait?" I didn't actually say anything, but Iain got the idea. "Evidently not."

SivSat might have exited the system by the other wormhole or even back through the one we'd just come through.

"How about this," I offered. "We go through the next wormhole in the direction of Adalans, and see what happens?" I pitched my voice in a way to make it sound like it would be fun, something that Iain could hardly pass up.

Iain rubbed his lips, then ended up with chin supported by his hand. "It's possible I can put my family off a few days. And get us to the wormhole quickly."

My smile was genuine, though I bet he didn't realize how much I'd played him.

Iain was able to coax our craft to more speed than I thought possible. The frigate would maybe catch up with us eventually. And then, we faced the wormhole that would take us to the last system before Adalans. We didn't wait till the night shift. I transited immediately. Again, traces of SivSat were detectable, which triggered a little quiver of excitement for me.

Nevertheless, the news was not all good. Along with the golden threads that trailed SivSat, there was also a thread of slimy concentrated darkness. Fortunately, I wasn't able to smell or taste it. Unfortunately, it had been through this portal.

KAG8? Never had I come across a feeling this bad. Some concentrated form of the rogue would make sense.

For safety's sake, I checked the scanner. The recently updated safeguards on our vessel's security were holding.

"Pearson. Pearson," I thought.

"Ajay?" he answered.

"Have you picked up any indications KAG8 is moving? Perhaps even its main body, or whatever would stand for its body. I just got a strong hint that it shifted to another system."

"Checking," responded Pearson. He took a really long time, perhaps three nano-seconds. "There does seem to be a movement in the data- nodes. This is news. KAG8 has never shifted physical position."

"Adalans," I thought. "It is going to Adalans."

"SivSatyananda?"

"I can only think so," I said. Prior to recently, KAG8 had worked only through its minions. Actually traveling somewhere seemed very risky. "Wonder if SivSat is on a mission regarding the new planet?"

"Perhaps," said Pearson. "Little information is available on how colonization of that planet is progressing, even among the computers. Someone is expert at keeping secrets."

❏❏❏

53 hours before self-destruction.

Chapter 26

Curiosity won out for Iain. Perhaps it was the story I'd told him of SivSatyananda disappearing in front of thousands at the Kumbh Mela, or that people a hundred years apart claimed to have seen the man, or that he was considered a mystical Master of Masters. Or maybe it was my excitement at the prospect of meeting SivSat. Whatever the case, Iain finagled his family into waiting till we returned from a trip to Adalans.

Turned out that not all of Iain's doubts were addressed, however. One afternoon, Iain challenged me. "From what you've mentioned, stopping KAG8 sounds impossible. What's your plan?"

I couldn't admit to Iain that, basically, I hoped SivSatyananda would fix it all by simple intention. Okay, maybe that was kind of optimistic, but my sense of SivSat was that any intention from him could move worlds.

An alternative might have been one of those special chants— the ones performed over many days and by the more pundits the better. They could fundamentally change things, even the course of physical events. Brahmaji had mentioned them back in my own time, and indications were that SivSat used them. But preparations for such performances took more time than we had—and that was even if SivSat could have been contacted beforehand and convinced of the need.

So, we'd just muck along the normal routes.

"Would 'praying for a miracle' be acceptable?" I asked in a tone designed to jolly Iain along. Clearly, that didn't work. "All right, then. Certainly we'll warn Callaghan about KAG8. And, if a fight breaks out, you'll probably command a battleship or something. As for me, I'll collect information on KAG8 to support that plan of attack." I neglected to mention that I'd send data to Pearson when Iain wasn't around—a practice that seemed to smooth sensitivities.

Iain remained unconvinced. "I think I'll draft a battle plan to discuss with Callaghan when we arrive."

Along the way, we visited stations and planets, most of which had already been checked by Pearson. It was chilling how KAG8 data-nodes appeared to be multiplying exponentially. I captured all the new ones, hopefully, and ignored the magnitude of data that somehow I'd have to pass on to Pearson.

On yet another space station, I dropped in at a bakery; the smell of fresh bread having grabbed my nose. While leaving— croissant in hand—a woman with a mop of red corkscrew curls just like mine caught my attention. Unfortunately, she was walking away and turned a corner before I could get a good look at her. I'd seen plenty of bottle-red locks in my new century, but not my thick curls, too. Kind of made me feel good, that I wasn't so completely different from everyone else.

As I turned to go back to the ship, a certain dignified gentleman left the same area where the redhead had been. This was the third time I'd seen this man, on as many stations along our route. Not only did I wonder if cloning had been perfected, but there was something familiar about him I still couldn't identify.

The man appeared to be in his fifties. Gray hair, strong jaw, steely eyes, impeccable clothes on a trim and fit physique that embodied "corporate chieftain." Before that instance, I'd only seen him in the middle distance—though it was hard not to notice him even then, he was that good looking. This time, however, he stopped in mid-stride and ogled me, from top to toe and back up. Not uncommon for men to notice me, though less so for someone so old and certainly being that obvious about it.

Reaching out to my lifeline, I found Pearson. After my description of the man, he said, "From now on, you need to be careful."

"Who is this guy?"

"That is not clear." His voice dropped an octave. "But the potential for dark circumstances seems to be strengthening in your chart." Before I could ask for more, he changed the subject. "I will arrive in the Adalans system shortly after you."

Huh. Didn't know he was also on his way to Adalans.

"Actually, that would help," I said. "It's not possible to transfer all the data we've collected via visual. How about if I leave it for you at the last space station before we transit through?" Pearson agreed, considering that by that time, him having the data was more important than secrecy.

Three days later and on the last station before Adalans, I was on my way back to the shuttle when who did I see on a huge news screen? Zaire Chevalier. Amidst all the competing news screens on the station, it was amazing I'd noticed him.

He delivered the news in serious-journalist speak. "Physicists identified a new particle, and their best guess is that it comes from the galactic core. Wags have dubbed this latest particle a Novatino," he said, modulating his voice to a slight comic tone. "More on how the Novatino may be related to the recently discovered shockwave on its way toward us, and how the particle seems to affect organic matter, when we return after this break."

I'd already accomplished my mission: leaving data packages for Pearson at two delivery companies.

Iain and I figured that if both of us left enough packages, even someone trying to waylay the data wouldn't be able to snag every single one. I hoped to walk back to the ship with Iain, so I settled in to hear more from Zaire.

Before the commercials were over, though, Iain entered the large common area from the other side of the station. I was about to wave to catch his attention when he paused and glanced around, as if someone nearby called his name. When the person came into view, my heart pounded. It was Turner Bishop, who seemed to get around a lot considering the last time I'd seen that sleaze was in Paris. Zaire and funny new sub-atomic particles zipped out of my brain.

Iain had mentioned months ago that he knew Bishop through business organizations, so I figured this might be just a friendly chat. After a few words from Bishop, however, it became clear that friendliness was not the intention at all. Iain almost raised a fist, as if to throw a punch.

Then Bishop said something and, yes, sneered. Iain turned and marched away, with Bishop laughing behind him.

At the entrance to another corridor branching off from the area, the dignified man I'd been noticing came to a stop, backed up to just barely around the corner, and then seemed to study Iain as he left. What Bishop did when he noticed the man was fascinating: Bishop abruptly focused on him, and then turned to almost scurry away.

Then the man did something that really grabbed my interest: he entered a restaurant. Forget Zaire—I now had a way to find out this man's name.

The restaurant he'd entered served fantastic popovers. In fact, lots of people loved those little pastry wonders, to the point that there was always a delay to be seated. Many times I'd left my name on a list at that restaurant's hostess station, like back in my old time. Only, in the present it was on a screen overseen by a robot.

Once the gentleman disappeared into the restaurant, I

nonchalantly scanned the area to see if I recognized anyone else in the area—friend or foe. No one.

Ambling in the direction of the restaurant, I kept track of the number of people entering: one person, a group of three, and then another individual. Eventually, I stood in front of the door. This food chain usually had a room where people could wait, though there was still a possibility the man remained near the door. I could risk going in to peek at the list, or I could scurry away like Bishop had and remain in the dark about this guy's identity.

The arrival of a couple of ladies simplified matters. I slipped in with them, quickly checking for anyone lingering nearby. Because the coast was clear, I waited for the hostess-bot to take care of the women. A casual lean on the podium near the bot allowed me a glimpse of the screen. "Yes, ladies," said the bot, "there is a twenty-five-minute wait. You may have a seat in that room there."

The ladies debated. Really, they had to expect the wait, since sometimes it was forty-five minutes for that restaurant. But their dithering was good. I got what I wanted. Almost for certain, the man's name was Fletcher.

I left before the bot had a chance to ask for my name. As soon as I got far enough away from the restaurant to take a deep breath, I decided to go back to a bakery with the smell of chocolate wafting from the open door. Iain's soft spot was chocolate chip cookies, and I could use some, too.

An hour later and onboard the frigate, Iain had nearly finished a whole bag of cookies.

I brought up the subject of his interaction. "For a moment there on the station, it looked like you were about to punch Turner Bishop." He stopped in mid-chew, so I continued.

"Which wouldn't necessarily be a bad thing, in my opinion."

He finished his cookie. "You saw," he said, sweeping away a crumb on his shirtfront.

"From across the common area."

Iain pondered the bag for a moment before responding. From the look on his face, I wasn't surprised when he went off topic.

"May I inquire, was it Pearson who gave you your dog?"

I could lie, but why? "Yes."

He nodded, and then seemed to carefully choose his words. "My esteemed business acquaintance during that delightful interlude on the station—besides some rather offensive language—implied something that helps explain many confusing instances." He glanced my way. "Is it possible that our mutual friend, the one who asked me to hire you and protect you, is...a robot?"

When I didn't immediately deny, he angled his head and dipped it in understanding. "Okay. So perhaps everything else implied was also true."

"What was implied?"

"Let's just say the sex trade is now very safe, since the 'workers' are incapable of passing on diseases."

"Oh, for heaven's sake," I snapped. "Is that all you guys can think of as a reason for a relationship with someone like Pearson? That's just pathetic, and a real surprise coming from you." Iain had the good grace to look rather ashamed. "You've been around him for more years than I have. In all that time, did you not receive genuine benefit from interactions with him, maybe even more than from humans? I know you must have."

Iain rubbed his face with both hands. "I concede your point. Yes. Pearson has been more trustworthy than many in my life. But please understand, I am from Varga. Though I've always enjoyed knowing about robots and how they work—more than anyone else in my family—the prejudice against such as Pearson is taught to us from an early age."

"Consider this then," I said. "Pearson is striking at the entity behind all the death and destruction, including..." I stopped, because it was clearly unnecessary to drive home the point about his brother. But I had to make sure Iain wouldn't go blabbing around about Pearson. "You also know how imperative it is for him to keep his secret."

"Perhaps I understand even more than you." He tapped his fingers on the arm of his chair. "His secret is safe with me."

I had to be satisfied with that. I wasn't going to ask him to cross his heart.

"Is a robot really the love of your life?"

Even for Iain, that was rather personal. I paused, with a cookie in my hand begging to be bit, and stared at the computer screen in front of me. Despite scrambled emotions about Iain hurling such a question at me, the answer popped into my head: no.

Okay, didn't know that.

I crammed the entire cookie into my mouth.

Pearson was certainly the one I owed the most to, however.

After minutes of silence between us, I left. An opening to ask Iain about the man watching him hadn't appeared, so that little mystery would have to wait. We both could use some alone time.

Later that shift, I detailed to Pearson the various places we'd left the data on the station. Our ships remained reasonably close, and it was good to have a normal conversation without long delays.

Then I warned him about Iain knowing about his robotic nature.

"Turner Bishop told Iain," I said. "Remember we tangled with Bishop on the Earth space station months ago? This afternoon, Iain asked me about it. I couldn't deny."

Because of my filament-slash-chip thing, I was seeing through Pearson's eyes. He was on the space station, and meandering through the corridors.

"Iain Newcastle knowing was inevitable. In fact, I had wondered if he had already guessed. Also, it was in the chart for something like that to happen today."

Pearson had begun explaining almost everything with Jyotish astrology, even to the extent of what someone ate for lunch. I gave in and asked, "All right, what's in my chart?"

His response was so immediate, he must have checked it recently. "Saturn is transiting your seventh house, and Rahu over your first house."

Strange as it may seem, it sounded familiar. "Rahu. You mean, as in a transit of the Jaguar god on Uxmal?" Nish had spent a whole evening instructing me on Uxmal's astrology, and another one about the beautiful cats on that planet.

As Pearson passed a glass storefront, I noticed him nodding.

"Master Irfanji mentioned Uxmal's astrological knowledge as real. Actually, in this situation, Jupiter in a specific beneficial position will save you. The Jaguar is stealthy, however. He may make an appearance."

"What about my father's chart?"

About half a minute passed before he said, "Danger near him, but he will prevail."

"And you?"

I was beginning to wonder if our connection had dropped.

"A major cycle appears to be completing for me."

"What cycle?"

"Saturn is transiting my twelfth house, also a solar eclipse over my ascendant."

"And that means?"

Again a long pause, then he said, "A completion."

"Completion of Mac's instructions regarding me? I can see how that could be. So, perhaps it's about beating KAG8?"

Pearson glanced at an electronics store window, and I looked back at him through his eyes. He smiled at me with only half his mouth. I was so distracted by the unusual smile that I barely noticed a person in the background in time.

"Pearson, bounty hunter coming at you from your left. Run!"

He immediately turned and hurried to the right, sprinting away. The area was crowded with shoppers and Pearson lost precious time by not simply barreling through. To be able to tell whether the bounty hunter was catching up, I switched to viewing the scene via the station's security cameras. As I watched, the man pulled out his laser. A couple of people near him jumped away when they noticed the weapon.

Pearson made a dash toward the dock where his shuttle waited, though he had to leave the relative safety of the crowd to do so. I kept skipping from one camera to another, trying to keep up with the chase. I had to remind myself to breathe.

"Halt!" bellowed the bounty hunter. "You are in violation of Varga Law 935C. This is your last warning." He shot at Pearson, and maybe grazed his shoulder.

Instead of taking the shortest route, Pearson opted to go back into a crowded area. Right outside the customs office, as a matter of fact.

Frantically trying to identify an edge for Pearson, I didn't at first realize robots had begun rolling into the bounty hunter's path in the corridors. It kept happening, each instance slowing the guy down. One time, he fell face first into a planter. I cheered. Pearson doubled back and practically dove into the float tube to his shuttle.

When he was safely in his ship I asked, "Pearson, did you call for help from those robots?"

He shook his head. "I do not know them, and they are not within my connections."

❑❑❑

31 hours 44 minutes before required commencement of self-destruct process.

Potential Response: Neutralize self-destruct programming.

Probability of success: 0.0008 percent.

Viable Response: Transfer KAG84950.301 to humanoid robot.

Chapter 27

The closer we got to the Adalans system, the more Iain frowned at the pad in front of him. Eventually, he began making notes. Since he hadn't talked about what was bothering him, at one point when he wasn't around I checked to see what the big deal was. The screen showed relative positions of ships in the vicinity. Nothing appeared abnormal.

The afternoon before we planned to transit through to Adalans, Iain muttered and marked up his pad.

"There is far too much traffic in this area," he declared, before contacting the station behind us. After some social chitchat, he asked about all the ships—tapping his foot the whole time—and cut the com- line afterward, pursing his lips. "Flight control says trade ship traffic has 'increased' and they sound proud of it. I hope they're right."

Unusual number of ships or no, we continued tagging along with the frigate. That night, the transit into the Adalans system cycled easily. Particularly so, since I picked up on the trail of SivSatyananda. The possibility of meeting him, at last, made me vibrate happily inside.

Unfortunately, there was also a strong hit of the evil of KAG8. Iain and those people on the frigate supposedly enjoyed a normal night's sleep. I got about an hour, because it took a long time to neutralize the residue of that exposure. KAG8 had traveled here for a reason. SivSat had to be its target.

Next morning, Iain and I transferred to the bridge on the frigate so he could make plans with the staff. About an hour later, the staff, including the first officer, had left the bridge and I was searching for data-nodes when Iain spoke up.

"How do you intend to locate SivSatyananda?"

"Whatever he wants in the Adalans system, the meetings would take place at the Temple on the planet. I thought we'd start there."

Iain's devilish grin should have been a warning. Considering his mood lately, he caught me by surprise with an offer full of implication. "Afterwards, perhaps we might take a stroll in the forest."

Couldn't help it, I chuckled, maybe even allowed a little flirtation in my smile at him. A walk shouldn't be a big deal. Nevertheless, the first time Iain and I met, on Adalans, he had insisted on following along with me on a walk through the woods. That I ultimately abandoned him on the path had clearly shocked him—poor boy wasn't used to such treatment. We had both tripped over half-truths on the forest path, him trying to romance from me the Key Crystal and me reeling from arrival in a new century.

I teased him back. "Or maybe this time I'll just lead you down the primrose path."

"Lead on, fair lady," Iain said, while moving his hand in a grand gesture.

Iain was being so normal with me, or more normal than he'd been since we began this mission, I began to relax.

Sadly, normalcy remained elusive—Pearson popped into my head, urgency fairly crackling in his connection. Trying my best to keep both of them happy, I thought, "Hi Pearson, just a minute."

Unaware, Iain continued. "Or we could locate a balsa wood plane, to fly through the Adalans skies."

Low blow! "And of course, you brought the gasoline."

"Alas, afraid not." The twinkle in his eye was real. "The last space station was all out. Perhaps next time we come across a certain ancient Cessna 195 airplane, I will be better prepared."

In my mind, Pearson interrupted.

"Ajay, a ship fired on the vessel belonging to the bounty hunter." His tone was urgent, nonplussed. Instantly I was pulled to Pearson's world. Who would fire on a ship belonging to an enemy of Pearson?

Iain chose that very moment to go all serious.

"Alexa, I want you to know that I spoke absolute truth that day we met on Adalans. I was fascinated with your plane. And, well, the prospect of spending time with someone like you was also very attractive. All that was not simply about a mission from my family." His tone softened. "The moment you spoke to me..."

I was facing him, my eyes on him. But he must have realized my attention was divided, because he stopped. The earnest look on his face faded into resignation. His upper lip even curled momentarily. Before I could say anything, he turned and walked out of the room.

I thought, "Pearson, you safe?" Upon an affirmative, I replied, "I'll get back to you."

Iain seemed to be in no mood to pause for anything.

"Iain, please wait." Not until I drew near was it obvious he was reading a message. He finally stopped, his attention still on the pad in his hand. He glanced at me, crossing his arms. I pulled back my hand before touching him. "Are you okay?"

"Perfect. Everything is fine. I have no problem with the woman I'm sharing something with suddenly switching her attention to someone more fascinating. I admit, it's an unusual experience for me. But it's all right. Rest assured, I will not bother you in the future. I understand all this is not about me. And, above all else, it's important for you to be happy with the relationship...in your head."

From his tone, it was surprising that Iain didn't harp on the robot detail. "Callaghan wants a face-to-face to discuss best practices for the cruisers my family sold him."

He left without saying goodbye.

"Wait. Please wait."

Iain didn't turn back to look at me.

Standing in the corridor, I stamped—a couple of times. "Iain Newcastle, you are so used to getting exactly what you want." *And such a baby when you don't.*

Later, I sprawled on a chair in front of the screen replaying his shuttle's departure.

Bill asked, "What is wrong?"

Chin in my palm, I looked over at my dog. "Human emotions."

"Beyond certain expressions and specific smells, human emotions are a mystery."

I gazed at the wall. The emptiness of the bridge reminded me of my head. I needed to check back with Pearson. "Hello? You there?"

"Always."

A response that both complicated my life beyond measure, and made me happy. That he was safe meant everything. "Was the bounty hunter's ship hit?" The delay had increased.

"Yes, though only enough to slow it."

"Was the bounty hunter the only one on the ship?" And was I going to have to drag out the details?

"I verified with my scanners that he was the only one on board. Otherwise, I would have stopped to help. From the shots at his vessel, it appeared the intent was destruction."

"Is it possible someone is trying to protect you? Your guardian angel?"

I heard Pearson's smile when he replied, "It would be nice to attract the attention of an angel."

"What is the status now?"

"The bounty hunter is an unknown. My ships are on their way to the industrial planet. Soon I will take a shuttle to make my way independently. I will let you know if something changes."

Thirty minutes later, I needed a break from KAG8 nodes. With the frigate between Adalans and the wormhole station, it should be possible to use the special transmission crystal for speaking to my father. Unfortunately, it soon became apparent he was not in a location with access to a sibling crystal. We were only able to converse with considerable delays.

In Dad's first statement, he apologized for not having much time. "Too many indications of imminent attack."

"Attack! Are you safe?" I asked.

A full minute later, his response came back. "Are you in the Adalans system? If so, please go back. It's too dangerous here."

"Attacked by whom?" I asked, and waited.

"Pirates, I fear."

My heart plummeted. Had KAG8 found out about my connection to Pearson, and struck without delivering the usual taunting message?

More likely, however, KAG8 was stalking SivSat.

"Do you know if a holy man named SivSatyananda is visiting Adalans?"

Dad sounded excited. "Heard rumors of him!" Then he switched to what would really concern him. "The family is evacuated to a protected place. We are fine. Better for you to remain safe and not come here."

Too late for that.

❑❑❑

23 hours 12 minutes before self-destruction.

Hainrich Fletcher predicts human female will protect humanoid robot.

Response: Nullify human female.

❑❑❑

I went back to scanning for KAG8 nodes, and found far more than should be in a system as small as this. Iain's doubts about accomplishing the impossible kept nagging at me. To keep me company, I set a speaker on the control panel to broadcast conversations among the nearby space cruisers. Perhaps I was hoping for a heads-up about Iain returning.

"Ajay, we meet again."

The voice didn't come through the speaker. Even as I spun, the man wearing an orange robe was easily recognizable.

"Trotaka!"

Many months had passed since I'd last seen the monk standing in front of me. We had all been scrambling around in the small shack on the bank of the Ganges River. A scene came to mind of him taking Rachel's hands and both of them winking out of sight. Almost for sure, he'd used the same mysterious method of transportation to show up in front of me now. His smile carried the same peace and depth of consciousness I'd felt then.

"Hello, Ajay."

The pleasure in his voice affected me the same as when I'd first met the man. He radiated peacefulness and wisdom in a way I'd only ever experienced with Brahmaji.

I missed being around Brahmaji. Intensely.

"Good news," he said. "SivSatyanandaji offers you an opportunity to return to your time."

I jumped. "Are you kidding? Why? How?"

"Crystal Ceres is at risk. We must identify it, quickly. And because you saw it in your original time, you are perhaps the best person to do so."

"You know about that crystal? The last time I saw it was with Brahmaji, almost a thousand years ago."

"Knowledge of it has been passed down to us. Now, we are almost certain of its location. Nevertheless, circumstance keeps its identity a secret, and time is of the essence," said Trotaka. "If you are willing to assist, SivSatyananda will make certain, in the end, you are delivered to your desired time."

Though back flips might have technically been beyond me, I was practically doing them. "So, everything would be as it was?"

"Correct."

Eyes closed, head back, my mouth opened for a silent shout. *All of this wouldn't have happened!* No crash landing in my grandfather's plane on some strange planet; no fleeing from robots and pirates bent on my destruction. I quietly exhaled.

Mac! His strong jaw and big grin, looking at me over his messy desk. At the possibility of running to his waiting arms, a small sob escaped me. Also tears, no matter how tightly my eyes were closed.

Even more on the plus side: No Penelope. No Varshana Vagwhatar. And certainly no Woolsey.

The blooming happiness in my heart paled a little when I realized, of course, no wormhole piloting either. Staring at a small rip on the station seat in front of me, I sighed. *Oh well, I'll never know the difference.*

Alas, also no Edith Holmes-Fong, with her warbling voice and devotion to her husband, Ghengis.

Still, I'd have Rachel, who would be as good a friend as ever, because she'd never have a chance to marry Mac. *What if I found out about the rendezvous between Rachel and Mac in that bar?*

Oh, dear. My throat went all thick. Dad. I'd never see him again, or meet my brothers and sisters. A sudden tension just wouldn't ease, no matter how I rolled my head or stretched my neck. I'd never know how much my father had missed me, how hard he'd tried to return to me. Lifting my chin a bit, I searched for a silver lining.

No KAG8! With the relief, I think my smile was a little shaky. *Well, that seals the deal.*

Hang on, probably no Pearson either. I massaged at the weight in my chest while wondering whether Mac would ever go to that much trouble, if I didn't disappear into the mists of the future. Even if Mac created Pearson for some reason, I wouldn't live to see how he developed so brilliantly. Never witness him crashing the boundary between human and machine, a robot's program reaching for the soul. My throat closed.

And no Iain Newcastle; arrogant, source of much exasperation, almost endearing, fountainhead of charm.

On the other hand, Mac...*who lived his life just fine without me.*

I faced Trotaka, who waited, no expectation, no hurry.

What about Pearson going off to do battle with KAG8, and Iain probably electing to take part in any fight?

"If I leave now, how would the present be affected?" The possibilities bubbled in my head. "I guess KAG8 would not even be created and all this wouldn't be happening. Therefore I wouldn't be missed?"

"Everyone here would continue—life would continue. You used a name, KAG8, of which I know not. On the other hand, many are searching for the Crystal Ceres."

Therefore, there could—almost certainly would—be some other crisis, or crises.

"Would Ceres be important now, whether I was here or not?"

"SivSatyananda has a mission for this century, and Ceres is crucial," said Trotaka.

"What would happen to everyone I've come across, if I was to be gone?"

"They would live their lives, just as you will live yours."

Inside, I was not jumping up and down and saying, *yes let's do it*, which was confusing.

"Do we have to go now? I mean, since it's time travel, we don't have to worry too much about leaving at this exact moment, right?"

Trotaka considered for a moment, head slightly to the side, before responding. "The undertaking is time sensitive. However, if you desire to remain in this particular 'now,' which is understandable, there is another way."

He'd offered me an alternative. Did I want to take it? "Do you mean that I won't ever get the opportunity to return to my time? If I decline, will SivSat be angry at me?"

He smiled. "SivSatyanandaji is never angry. And he is capable of many miracles. On the other hand, once the Crystal Ceres is located, I am almost certain his attention will be on using it for good."

Thus, my attempts to keep the option of going back in time available for my whim were undeniably self-centered.

I could leave. I could go home. It could all work out and no one would know. Maybe not even me.

"Is SivSat on Adalans? Perhaps he's here regarding your new planet?" I dearly wanted to talk to SivSat; find out what would be the right action.

Trotaka gazed at me kindly. "He departed."

I waited, hoping for more information.

From the background crackles sounding from the speaker, a note of panic emerged. Garbled words clarified into an announcement that the total of unknown ships in the system had recently surged. Callaghan's forces were stretched between Adalans and the industrial planet. Considering that the planet was a source of all the crystals used by humans in propulsion, communications, and hovering craft, it was a rich prize for any pirate. Every instinct told me the Adalans system would soon be under attack.

If I left, part of me would know. And judge me wrong.

Chapter 28

Sitting in a chair on the frigate's bridge, I was quietly coming to grips with my choice with Trotaka when the com-panel lit up. Someone hailed the ship, using the equivalent of all caps to do so.

I depressed the button to accept the call. A man's voice sounded, commanding, "Get the captain on the line." An indicator showed the connection was routed through the station's special transmission crystals. Four seconds later, an image came up.

The man gazed at me with as much surprise as I felt.

"Get me Iain," said Lord Hadrian Newcastle, Iain's oldest brother and the same man who had glared at me as I crossed the throne room in New Britain.

"Iain is on his way to a meeting on another ship. May I have him return your call?"

"I will contact this ship again in thirteen hours. If you do not alert him, there will be consequences."

Iain had implied his elder brother was extraordinarily controlling. "To my knowledge, messages on this ship are always delivered. Particularly to Iain."

"We will see. You have thirteen hours." With that, Lord Newcastle signed off.

Oh, boy.

I was considering my good luck in not having an older sibling when Callaghan contacted the ship via a video link. Much closer. No time lag.

This was the first time I'd laid eyes on Callaghan since leaving Adalans many months ago. Despite our mutual pleasure in seeing each other, it was obvious he was worried.

"Lass, grand to glimpse your bonny face. I look forward to hearing more of the adventures your father told me about." His next statement explained his concern. "Do you ken where is Iain?"

"He's supposed to be with you."

"Yes, Iain's last message said he was on his way. He never showed up." I turned to the control panel to locate Iain. Callaghan continued, "And there has been no response to our messages since."

I tried pinging Iain anyway, despite a sudden dizziness.

"Perhaps waylaid by an old friend?" I asked. "They're everywhere, you know." *Especially women.*

"I'd be surprised. It appeared Iain understood the urgency. We will try broadcasting around the station, and I'll let you know."

I got no response from Iain, which would only happen if he was engrossed in something, *whatever that might be.* In the silence after Callaghan signed off, I verified Iain had actually left the ship and which shuttle he took. There was even a video of him boarding and the backside of the craft as it headed in the correct direction. I tapped into the space station's surveillance system. Really, if Iain had decided to hook up with one of his girlfriends... not sure what I'd do, but it would be fierce.

Unfortunately, no Iain showed up on the station videos in the relevant time period. A heaviness clamped down around me.

Callaghan hailed the ship. The look on his face didn't inspire optimism.

"Iain's shuttle has been located. No one is responding from it. We are on our way to intercept." Callaghan signed off.

It would have been nice if people were on the bridge, but they were all off working on instructions from Iain. While waiting for word back from Callaghan, I searched desperately for some kind of explanation: Transferred to a friend's ship? Decided to take a space-walk? I veered off the thought of him being forced into a space-walk.

An interminable hour later, it turned out that the shuttle was two-thirds of the way to the station. Empty. The shuttle betrayed no sign of struggle. Callaghan's men even searched within a reasonable distance from it and the station, a hunt I knew was for a body. Still nothing. I tried to keep panic at bay. Bill leaned against my leg.

After Callaghan signed off from delivering all available information, I gave in and reached out to my safety net. "Pearson?"

Almost a minute later I felt his presence in my head and responded over his words, unable to contain my concern. "Iain never made it to a meeting with Callaghan." From the silence on the other end, Pearson was as shocked as me. After relaying the details, I asked, "Could it have been KAG8?"

"I do not think so. There would have been a body."

A body. I shouldn't panic, because there wasn't a body. At least that's what everyone was saying. Worried and helpless and not willing to admit to how much, I switched subjects. "You were saying something when we first connected?"

"I detect a potential plan of attack. The unidentified ships are stringing themselves out between Adalans and the other planet."

"Dad told me he heard rumors of SivSat in the system."

"Which would explain much."

"Yeah, I am almost certain KAG8 is here," I said. "Picked up on it while transiting through the wormhole." I wondered why KAG8 remained in the system. But I wasn't going to tell Pearson that SivSat had departed. The only way I could know that would be via someone like Trotaka. How could I explain to Pearson that I had again refused to take the action his entire existence was designed to make happen? Not necessary, at least right then.

Pearson said, "I am preparing to begin the program that will neutralize the KAG8 nodes. Before that, however, I will block transmissions out of this system. This may cause challenges for the Adalans forces, but it will also disallow KAG8 from mustering its resources to quickly reconstruct."

The nodes all had to go at the same moment, or as close as possible, without alerting KAG8.

Later that day, I hung out on the bridge. Theoretically I was checking for more data-nodes, though really I was waiting for any news about Iain or from Pearson. Bad went to worse when chatter among the ships told of more potentially hostile vessels on the other side of the wormhole. Callaghan urged me to move the frigate away from it.

"Despite the mystery of Iain's disappearance, no violence in the shuttle is a good indication, because Iain would not have given up without a fight."

If I left, Hadrian would have trouble contacting the ship. In a way, I'd love to avoid that impending conversation. But remaining available to Hadrian would be the right thing to do, and probably better in the long run. On the other hand, the frigate would be in a direct line of fire from anyone barreling through the wormhole. After discussions with the frigate's first officer, we opted to move in the direction of Adalans, at a slow speed.

Really, I can be incredibly dense at times. Not until the middle of the night did it occur to me where Iain had gone, or with whom. Trotaka had said, *if you desire to remain in this particular 'now,' there is another way*. Was Iain the other way? My teeth clenched. Wouldn't it be perfect irony for Iain to end up in my time, instead of me?

As well, those tense moments between Iain and Turner Bishop came to mind. Bishop could also be at the bottom of this mystery. I rolled out of bed and turned on my pad, searching for traces of Mr. Bishop in the news.

By the time for the call from Iain's brother, I'd gotten no sleep. Even so, I showed up at the appropriate time near the com-panel on the bridge. A ping indicated an incoming call. The face on the video was not happy to see me.

Hadrian barked, "I specified Iain. Such orders usually do not include others."

"Lord Newcastle, I am very sorry to tell you this...but Iain is missing."

Despite the man's rude manner, concern on his face betrayed real caring for Iain. His next words made quite clear his opinion of me, however.

The man spoke in clipped words. "Not only have you bewitched Iain into putting your wishes before the company's, but by insisting on this harebrained detour, evidently his very sense of self-preservation is addled, too! What have you done with him?"

I opened my mouth a couple of times, trying to figure out how to respond.

"Nothing," I managed. "When you called yesterday, he'd left for a meeting with Murdoch Callaghan. Shortly after your contact, Callaghan informed me that Iain never showed up for the meeting."

"We will see about that." He reached and hit at something and the connection dissolved. I was a high school kid sitting outside the principal's office.

Hadrian's words to me later were not far off the mark.

"You will leave our ship immediately. I have commanded the

first officer to take you to the nearest station. Your employment contract is ended. Whatever wages owed to you will be deposited into your account, despite everything." He reached to end the contact.

"Wait!" I yelled. Once verified the man actually remained on the line, I demanded, "What is going on?"

Hadrian scowled at me as if I were an enemy agent.

"Our family was notified of your status. With what Master Wormhole Pilot Woolsey told us, I am surprised you didn't lose the entire ship in a wormhole transit. Leave now, or prepare to defend yourself against a suit." He broke contact.

Stunned, instinct urged me to check my mail. I'd been ignoring it. Evidently a bad idea. After sifting through the rubbish in the list, I finally located an official missive from a month ago. It was a notification to stop transiting through wormholes while the Pilot Board considered charges brought by Woolsey.

I might have made a wrong decision with Trotaka.

❑❑❑

10 hours 3 minutes before mandatory self-destruction.

Chapter 29

Lord Hadrian Newcastle decreed the frigate would be turned into a warship and handed over to Callaghan. Before that, however, the staff unloaded me at the nearest station, which happened to be the one above Adalans. They were apologetic, but thorough.

Thus, late in the morning and perched on a pile of my belongings in an empty cavernous dock on the station, I was unsure about what to do. Bill guarded me, against what was not clear.

Pearson, who had sent his fleet toward the industrial planet before striking out on his own, needed to know my location, at least to be aware that I wasn't able to continue searching for nodes. I left his computer on the ship, though took the program and all its data with me.

I barely waited for him to greet me.

"Iain's brother threw me off the ship." Pearson's confusion was palpable. I explained, "My most solicitous adversary, the Right Irrational Pilot Ellis Woolsey, managed to strike at the worst possible moment. I am presently barred from transiting wormholes, and Hadrian Newcastle thinks I foisted myself onto Iain and may have lost him in a wormhole transit."

Pearson wasn't alarmed. "A misunderstanding that can certainly be rectified later. In the meantime, Nicholas left one of my ships at the station."

There had been no indication of any other ship on our approach. In fact, the station appeared deserted. "At what dock? It's not nearby."

"My people are trying to contact Nicholas."

To locate the ship left by Nick, I needed to check the docking areas. To my knowledge, the station had not been declared enemy territory. It had simply been abandoned by most humans for the relative safety of the planet.

Tugging my backpack into place, I got my bearings. From the exit into the station, Bill warned, "Robots are nearby." Probably he was referring to the normal high whine of a couple of cart-bots tooling along on the other side of those double doors.

"Maybe not a problem, but we should be careful."

"I will protect you," said my Chihuahua.

"Thank you. Keep me informed about the robot situation. Try to not let them know about you. Okay?" In answer, he cut his eyes over to me. Probably didn't need to ask him to keep in touch with Pearson. I hoped, however, Pearson wouldn't split his computing power to work through Bill.

We were on the space station I'd visited when I first arrived in this century. Twice, I'd walked through the exact hangar we were in, though both times I'd been overwhelmed and hadn't noticed the layout of the other docks.

No help from Adalans. On our way to the station, ship chatter confirmed the planet was without power. The hour they realized the number of pirate ships arriving in system, Callaghan had ordered people to sail away on the ocean with the huge central crystal.

Before checking outside the doors I asked Bill, "Robots in the hallway?" He said no. A quick peek into the corridor showed that its empty curve followed the station's spherical shape. Also, on our right there were two sets of double doors, which implied a similar hangar space as we were in. Possibly more doors existed further along the corridor, though the curve hid them.

The station almost certainly had more hangars; I just had to locate them.

Bill gazed up at me. "I can check out the nearby spaces."

A mental image of the robot aiming to smash Bill to pieces remained clear for me. Despite us ultimately beating the bot, I wasn't willing to put Bill in that kind of danger again.

"Tell you what, let's start with the corridor and see what happens."

On the way to a station map, we passed four cart-bots. The last one stopped after it passed us, turned its head in our direction, and then zipped away. My hackles bristled at the sounds of people running in adjoining corridors. Bill strode beside me, daring anyone to come close.

An entrance to a large area showed the kitchen court, which appeared empty, offering no possibility of food. No one was in the area. Correction: as I watched, one person strolled across the open space. It was Fletcher, looking as sophisticated and urbane as he did all the previous times I'd seen him. He paused in the middle and checked out the askew tables and chairs. Plates and leftovers had been cleaned away. Little else had been tidied up before everyone fled. Fletcher approached the kitchen under the sign advertising Chinese food, craning to see into the back while sniffing for telltale aromas. He continued his tour, turning down a corridor I remembered as being full of offices. I wasn't going to offer my services as a tour guide.

Bill and I scooted to the next hallway, aiming to follow the outside of the station. Though all was calm, I could practically feel the violins shrieking in the background. Despite such hyper-awareness, however, a high whine approaching the corridor from the kitchen court barely gave me enough notice.

I had jumped behind a planter and ducked down, but that didn't mean the bot didn't shoot at me. First a smell of hot metal filled the area, then part of a long leaf floated onto my head. Shortly after that, the same high whine retreated from the hallway entrance.

Instead of going with the instinct to curl up behind the planter, I forced myself to stand up and bolt.

"Bill!" He ignored me and strode toward the corridor entrance. I turned. "Bill! Come with me!" He remained there, staring at the empty passageway—empty for the moment. "Bill, come now!" Really, dogs with big intellects can be a problem.

He galloped over. "The robot shot at you, which is disallowed according to base programming in every robot." He seemed personally offended at such an overt challenge to the basis of all bot-kind.

If robots were attacking, KAG8 had hacked them. I needed a laser of my own.

"We'll report it later. First, let's find our ship." A curve in the hallway gave me hope we might be on the right track.

First we crept slowly, then dashed, then slowed again, me straining my ears every step of the way. Nothing prepared me for being slammed by a belligerent vacuum cleaner, however. A butler-bot, my nemesis almost from the beginning, finally showed its true colors. Right before the end of the corridor, all I saw before being smacked in the face was a bunch of tubes click-clacking its way out of a room to our left. Nothing amusing about the scenario, though, because the beast immediately threw itself at my head, trying to gouge at my eyes. I yelled and kicked.

Bill yanked on a hose, his tug-of-war prowess paying off.

At long last, we forced the bot back and I slammed the door. Bill barked wildly.

"Shhhh! Bill, we need to be quiet. Don't want to attract attention."

As we slipped away he got in a final word, though, when he gave a low guttural *hmmrph*.

We went through two open areas without incident, except for news screens that showed pictures of fire-engulfed buildings on Adalans. I had to trust my father was right about a safe place for him and the family.

With no robots in sight, I began to hope they were busy elsewhere. The next hallway proved me wrong. Two cart-bots and a third one looking like R2D2 bore down on us. The high whines provided some notice, but no door would open to allow us into a safe room. I snatched up Bill and flat-out ran.

Right into the arms of a human. The man must have heard my frantic steps, because otherwise we'd all be in a pile on the floor.

"Whoa there. Which ones are after you?" He quit asking dumb questions when a laser shot came way too close. Guess he knew what he was doing, because before I opened my mouth, three fried robots smoked in the hallway. "Been playing tag with bots for hours. Never seen anything like it."

It was the bounty hunter.

"What are you doing here?" I demanded.

"Need to get my ship repaired. There are precious few humans on this station, so I could ask the same question of you." He cocked his head, requiring an answer. Biceps muscled out from under a short-sleeve shirt. Maybe he'd shaved a few days ago, which fit with the bushy graying hair pulled back in a short tail.

"None of your business." Bill punctuated my statement with a growl.

The man's glance said I was way ungrateful. Then he did a double take. "Wait. I've seen you before." He took me by the shoulders and moved me from side to side. "Yeah, you were with the bot in the hotel room. Do you know it's a robot?" He jeered, "Or maybe you do. I understand that type can perform in certain extra-special ways."

I was *not* going in that direction. "You have no idea what you're doing. You're only a hired gun."

"This gun just saved your butt." He scanned the area. "The android's nearby, isn't it? I got a tip."

"Forget about it. I'm here to stop the real problem behind this invasion."

"Oh yeah? How're you going to do that?"

"Again, none of your business," I said.

"Let me get this straight, you just happen to be on an abandoned space station, out for a stroll."

"Looking for my ship."

"Only one remaining is on the other side," he said, pointing back the other way.

Gak. I'd gone the wrong direction.

He offered, "I can take you there."

"No. Thank you."

His laughter didn't help much. "Your hide, princess."

As he marched off in search of more robot target practice, I muttered, "I am not a princess." I put Bill on the ground and fished out from the heap of metal the one laser not destroyed by big, brave Mr. Bounty Hunter.

Should I continue hugging the perimeter? Or cut across? Cutting across would probably save time—or get me very lost. I should have taken the guy up on his offer. Sometimes I was such a screw-up. Should have just stayed in one place, and waited for Pearson. *Wonder how far back to where the frigate dropped me off that morning?*

"Too far," came the answer inside my head. My voice. Not Pearson's.

Sometimes in a confusing situation, asking a simple question in my head would deliver the right answer. I asked, *Keep going around the station?* "No."

Across? No answer. Hate it when that happens.

Is it safe to go across? "No."

Will I find what I want if I go across? "Yes."

Will I find what I want if I keep going around? No answer.

Would I be the stupid person in the movies who goes where everyone in the audience knows is trouble? Or play it safe and maybe not get where I needed to go.

Images flickered in my mind: fires engulfing the beautiful guesthouses where I stayed months ago on Adalans, threatening all those wonderful people.

Right. Stupid it is.

It wasn't possible to carry Bill and keep the laser ready, so I leashed him and began doing an imitation of a guerrilla fighter.

The first time I fired the laser I nearly dropped it afterwards. Not that there was a kick from the weapon, nor did it deaden my hearing. And not that I was a bad shot. In fact, one time back in Florida when practicing with high school friends at their family's ranch, I turned out to be the best shot. Also the only one to wear earplugs in addition to earmuffs. The bot coming at us was far more humanoid than any little tin cans set up for our target practice, though.

When the robot dropped after my shot, I swear it screamed. I didn't go over to put it out of its misery, if it really was experiencing pain. I simply fled. *Note to self: ask Pearson about bots and pain.* Bill bounded beside me, amazingly stoic. He'd leaned against my leg when the bot went down.

According to the maps, we'd made it a little over halfway across the station. On the other side of the open area in front of me, four corridors branched off in roughly the correct direction and came together again some way further on. Bending low while also trying to stay on the lookout for rogue robots, I rushed toward the hallways.

Too soon, a volley of laser shots forced me to the floor.

One bot came at me, shooting as it trundled along. A hot pain lit up my arm. I followed what all the military television shows taught: roll away and bring up my firearm. After I got off one shot and before I rolled again, Bill dashed and made a super leap at the bot—higher than any I'd seen, even to grab the end of a rope.

I kept tumbling and finally got to the point where I was able to maneuver to my knees and onto my feet. Another robot came at us. It started then stopped, started then stopped. A shot or two from me brought it to a halt. Dashing for the safety of the corridor, I called out, "Bill, come now!"

In the dive into the corridor, a shot nearly singed my behind, which would have balanced the pain on my arm. From behind another planter, I glanced around.

"Bill?" Dear God, he wasn't with me. "No."

I eased from around the planter. Another robot took a wild shot at me, hitting the top of the tree. I fired back, and it turned off in another direction. Ten seconds later, a peek into the large area showed me Bill, fifteen feet away. Down and not moving.

Sometime later, I have no idea how long, innumerable robots and robot parts littered the common area. Circuits sputtered, smoke from electrical fires curled in the air—sharp, acrid.

I crouched in an HVAC duct with Bill in my arms, reluctant to again glimpse his damage. The overheated laser lay beside me.

Rocking, rocking, I cradled him. Or myself, hard to tell. No sound escaped me, because robots prowled at the grate.

Chapter 30

"Ajay?"

Awaking with a start, I nearly cried out. Air rushed around me as the HVAC system did its job, chilling my chest under a damp shirt. I had to stifle an urge to cough. The smell of burnt wires lingered. The voice inside my head belonged to Pearson.

Fingering Bill's ears, I responded, "I'm here."

"I lost track of you." He probably meant to say he'd lost track of Bill. My responding thoughts were the only strong thing about me.

"I'm out of this, Pearson. I'm done. You and the world and the galaxy will have to go on without me." His reaction was silence; Bill was more his child than mine. "I'm sorry, Pearson. I failed. I didn't keep him safe. He tried to protect me, and succeeded. And now—"

An alarm went off somewhere, perhaps on the other side of the common area. I took advantage of the noise to let out a sob. Though had to dam the flood when a high-pitched whine approached.

"Ajay."

I gulped, swallowed, tried to push it all down. "Bill is gone!"

Pearson waited for a bit. "There is a backup."

The offer of a potential solution froze me in place. Eyes darting, I avoided sight of the body in my arms.

"Pearson, this vessel is very damaged."

"Remember our conversation about reincarnation?" I nodded, though of course he couldn't see. "Even with biological bodies, which are impossible to repair, you have seen how second chances come around. All may not be lost." His voice was strong and soft at the same time. I hiccuped.

"However, an opportunity for that is slim," he said. "After a test shutting down wormhole transmissions, KAG8 seems to sense my intentions. And the auspicious time for bringing all this to an end is almost upon us."

"I am useless, Pearson," I bawled. "Nothing I do would stop this process."

"The ship left behind by Nicholas has a laser cannon. You would have to activate the connections, but it is available."

He allowed me a moment to salvage myself; an interval, to locate even a shred of intention.

□□□

2 hours 48 minutes before mandatory self-destruction.

Chapter 31

What I could actually do with a laser cannon would become clear if I ever got to it. In the meantime, I needed to deal with the pissed-off robots on the hunt for me.

Pearson and I managed to identify the probable hangar for the ship, after he referred to the last message from Nicholas. My mission to traverse to the correct quadrant for the ship and claim it for the good guys was straightforward, if not straight. Corridors in my current quadrant meandered to and fro, implying some makeshift craftsmanship in the past to connect various ships into a station.

I walked by another vid screen with what seemed to be live pictures, perhaps from automatic cameras aimed at the planet from here on the station. In fact, the graininess implied a viewpoint from this station, which meant the flames were scary high. A ship passed in front of the camera, strafing a village—all those people who'd been so hospitable to me when I first arrived. *Okay, gotta get there. Soon.*

The air intake vent where I'd taken refuge with Bill had been kind of big, and such ductworks were more likely to go in straight lines.

"The vents may be big enough for me, Pearson. Do you have a schematic for this station?"

It took him a bit to respond, and for us to conclude that me scooting through a few tight places would cut off a good chunk of the maze.

⌒ᐞ×

So far, so good. Kind of.

"How are you doing?" inquired Pearson.

He hadn't checked in on me for at least five minutes. It might

229

have been the way I yelled at him, while dragging myself through metal places designed for utility bots. Bill was in my backpack, which I'd tied to my ankle.

At the moment, I was above an open area, looking down through a grill.

"The bounty hunter is on the station. He's working with a few others, chasing down robots." As I watched, he shot again. "Just demolished another." Some bots were frozen in place. The bounty hunter jogged away, heading the opposite direction from my destination. Good.

"It is possible someone on my staff has been providing my locations," said Pearson. "Which is why I am not on my freighter."

Fletcher watched the proceedings from the side, and I realized why he seemed familiar.

"Remember that older man I told you about? I think his name is Fletcher. And strangely enough, he looks rather similar to Iain." A bot searched the space up near me, probably because my foot had clanged recently. After it gave up and continued on its way, so did I.

Pearson was quiet for a moment, which was good because I needed to squeeze through a tight space.

"The maiden name of Iain's mother is Fletcher," he said. More silence as I kept pulling myself along. "Hainrich Fletcher is an uncle of Iain's."

"Do you know anything about him? He's on this station."

"Mr. Fletcher is a medical doctor who no longer practices medicine, but has become a successful businessman."

Iain Newcastle was complicated, and it would behoove me to run the other way if—*when*—he surfaced again.

Three times I had to transfer from one duct system to another. Two went without a hitch, while the one in the middle resulted in another fried bot. I hated the feeling, even considering what they'd done to Bill or that my own skin was at risk.

At the nearest I could get to my destination—still a couple of docks away—I sat in the duct work and tried to sense if any bots were nearby. Sounded safe. I pushed against the grill. No give, no movement. It took some effort in the tight confines, but finally I shifted, bent double, turned into position, and kicked. The clamor as the grill dropped to the ground echoed through the halls.

Good thing I paused, because almost immediately a horde of cart-bots approached the corner. Shuffling back in, I brought the grill up barely before the first of about eight bots rounded the corner. With the slats pointed down, only their wheels were visible. On the other hand, that was probably why they didn't detect me. As a unit they stayed in place, silent. I moved not a muscle, except for my heart banging against the metal around me. One bot had stopped particularly close in front of my grate, its laser held at the ready, right in front of my eyes. They waited for about a decade, while I sweated. Good thing bots generally didn't have good smellers.

Perhaps even robots get bored, because eventually they moved on. Still I waited, checking my bracelet phone for the time. When a little over thirty minutes remained before the auspicious time period for Pearson to begin his routine, I pushed out the grate, laid it down gingerly, and dashed for my target.

A man jumped out at me from behind the first dock along my path. I about had a heart attack. Lucky for him, he yelled enough for me to get past my hyped up fight-or-flight response. It's possible he was responding to the laser pointing at him.

"Princess! It's me, Nish." He held his hands out toward me, his eyes betraying fear.

I considered whopping him on the head.

"Nish? What are you doing here?"

"Princess, your father the king sent me." He took hold of my hand and drew me toward the nearest hangar. Not where I was heading. Yet there was a real probability of more murderous cart-bots rolling our way. After the doors closed, he said, "To take you home."

Florida? Uxmal? "Home? What home?"

Nish bobbled his head like one of those little felt-covered animals in the back of some cars.

"Here. Adalans is home now. Come, we must leave." He continued pulling me to a departure iris.

"Leave with you?" I dug in my heels, and at least slowed the forward momentum. "I don't think so."

"Yes, Princess. You must."

"No, Nish. I won't."

"Yes."

"Uh. No." His response was to simply start trying to pull me toward the iris. "Stop. I can't go with you. I appreciate my father's concern, but I have a job to do."

"You are in danger. I can tell. You are carrying a laser, which is not appropriate for a princess, ever. You must come." He began pulling again. "Come."

Practically being dragged across the hangar, I shouted, "Nish. Stop." He didn't. I yelled, "I command you to stop." At least he paused. "I won't go with you. You must go and tell my father I am fine."

Nish responded by bringing out the big gun, a communicator directly to my father.

"Alexa? Are you there?" My father's voice filled the space.

Why can't it ever be easy? "Dad?"

"Alexa! Excellent, Nish found you. He knows where to bring you. Few places are safe now."

"Dad, I'm not coming with Nish."

To disprove my words, Nish began dragging me again. I yanked my hand from his. "Tell Nish to cease and desist or I will go crazier than you ever saw me as a teenager." When my father didn't immediately respond, I said, "Not kidding." The up-voice at the end was not a question mark.

"Nish, would you mind giving my daughter and me a few moments, please?"

"Yes, King Johnalden." Nish walked by himself toward the iris. "Alexa, what is the problem?"

"I have a job to do. It's important. It will help protect you and many others."

He was quiet on the other end for a moment. "Do you have to be in the middle of the fray? I went to great effort to arrange a place with electricity for the children; for you. With this, you can communicate anywhere."

I fought the guilt trip. "Dad, thank you. You always take such good care. But in this case, I have to go my own way." After a beat, I said, "On my own terms."

Silence again. The clock was ticking. I had just declared independence from my father, and regardless of how appropriate it was, considering everything, he needed to process.

"Go. Do your job. Be safe." His voice didn't actually choke up.

"Thank you, Dad. You be safe, and all the kids."

Had to go, time was flying. Nish rushed over and I handed him the communicator. Bolting toward the doors, I yelled over my shoulder to my father, "Love you!" After verifying I wouldn't rush into the arms of a cart-bot in the corridor, I sprinted to the correct hangar.

Only after blasting through those doors did I see the butler-bots, a hundred of them. Okay, maybe closer to forty. Even so, access to the iris to Pearson's ship was guarded by a platoon of butler-bots, all of them advancing on me.

I'd been relatively nice to those creepy little robots in the past, by simply escorting each one out of a room. Not this time. I kicked, and booted, and punted. Parts and tubes flew. Some grabbed my pants, so I whacked their beady little eye orbs. Others tried to trip me, and I mowed them down into each other with my arms. One particularly vicious bot had wrapped its vacuuming tube around my leg. I had to stop and unwind it, which of course left my back open to attack from another.

A human waded into the fray. It was Nish. And I must say, he kicked butler-bot butt. Finally, the tide turned.

When knee deep in butler-bots, it's good to remember the goal. In this case, not to drain the swamp but to get into the ship. I leaped over two bots lifting up their vacuum units at my head, and slammed my hand on the control to open the iris. When just barely enough space opened up for me, I dove through. Then Nish. Some witnessing element in my mind wondered how I would get Nish back to his ship. First we had to neutralize the bots, though.

Various butler-bot appendages began snaking their way through the iris, trying to catch us or follow along. I hit the iris control to get it shut. It whined, but couldn't close completely. Abandoning that idea, I pushed off toward the ship's door.

"Pearson! Code. Need the code!" I knew it was useless.

Chapter 32

Butler-bot noises closing in on me ensured that I didn't debate over the shuttle door suddenly opening.

Only after squeezing through and making certain Nish secured the door, did I realize Mr. Bounty Hunter waited for me, grinning.

"You're about as subtle as colliding asteroids."

"Get off this ship."

His gun was bigger than mine, though happily not aimed at me. "And allow in the butler-bots waiting on the other side?"

A glance at a monitor proved him correct. I bustled past him and pushed off toward the bridge, ignoring Nish who tagged along, almost touching me. I glared at the bounty hunter. "Buddy, you are not welcome on this ship. You have no right to be on this ship. You have no business on this ship."

"Name is Gus Magness. And actually, this is my business. Where you go, the android will likely be."

Really, about as bossy as my grandfather.

Nish asked, "What is an android?"

Refusing to grant a name to the hulking man in front of me, I said, "You are so brainwashed by idiocy."

He ignored Nish's question, too. "I have a job. What I believe about androids has nothing to do with it. Though I am good at recognizing someone who doesn't know she's the one who's been brainwashed."

"I will allow no one to brainwash the princess," said Nish.

Magness glanced Nish's way, then at me, and smiled. "See, I was right. You're a princess."

"No. I'm not." I fired up the control panel for the ship.

"Yes, she is," said Nish. "She is the daughter of King Johnalden."

"Did I hear that right? The king of God gas is your father?" He slapped his leg. "Oh, the story just gets better and better."

Yet another voice joined the fray when Pearson popped in my head.

"Ajay? Are you near the ship yet?"

"Just a sec, Pearson," I thought, and then fixed Nish with my steeliest stare. "We will stop at the dock next to your ship, and you are leaving." The bounty hunter hung off to the side, still cackling.

Back to Pearson in my mind, I said, "I'm on the ship. The bounty hunter is here, and one of my father's men." It would take over a minute to get a response from Pearson.

Nish hung close, though not close enough for me to swat him. As he was pointing out to me on a map where my father and the family was— indeed, no enemy ships were paying attention to that area—Magness decided to activate the navigation panel. I yelled at Magness, "What are you doing?"

"If you're going somewhere, high odds it's to the android. I'll help you."

"Princess, are you involved with an android? That sounds dangerous."

"Oh yeah," Magness said to him. "It's dangerous. And, you and her father should do everything possible to help me capture the android, so I can put it away forever."

I bore my eyes into the bounty hunter. "You shut up." I glared at my father's man. "Nish, don't listen to him. He's just doing this for money. And both of you," I swept my hand at them, "get out of my way."

Next to what had to be Nish's ship, considering the jaguar painted on the nose, was probably the bounty hunter's ship. Hard to miss the scorch mark running the entire length.

I turned to Nish. "This is it. Time to go."

When he didn't follow along, I reached back and grabbed his sleeve before pushing off toward the exit.

"Princess, your father wants me to stay near and protect you." As I continued dragging us both along the corridor, Nish continued protesting. "He said if you would not come to safety, it is my duty to bring it to you."

Less than fifteen minutes remained before Pearson would begin his routine to eradicate KAG8. In the shuttle, I punched the button to open the door, then verified the tube to the station was clear and the iris at the other end open. No butler-bots in front of us, or on any monitor.

Nish grabbed a handhold on the wall, and wouldn't let go. "Princess, your father commanded me to stay with you. He will be very angry with me if I return without you. Please do not make me leave."

I pulled on him, stretching to aim him at the door. "I don't have time for this, Nish!"

"But what if the pirates take you, too?" he wailed.

I felt about two inches tall, considering his wife.

Magness floated nearby, with a wiseass grin on his face. "Tell you what. You seem to be in a hurry, and I want to help you every way I can." He suggested, "Why don't you let me handle this?"

"Yes. Get him onto the station. You have twenty seconds." I pushed off back toward the bridge.

Before firing up the engines, I verified the outside door was sealed, the tube was empty and disconnected, and the iris into the station closed. Our engines may have singed the station.

Magness floated into the bridge in time to see me entering the pilot pod. He asked, "Are we transiting out of system?"

Nice that he'd at least assumed I was a wormhole pilot. "Anything to get you out of here. You can make yourself useful by getting the laser cannon up and running." He didn't bother me with questions about details. Guess a bounty hunter could be useful for something.

I locked the pilot pod's door behind me, took off my backpack containing Bill, and secured it at my feet.

"Pearson. I'm in the ship. I can't get rid of the bounty hunter. How can I help?"

The delay had become painfully long. He had to be almost at the other side of the system.

"If you can identify the location of KAG8, that would be helpful," he said. "Otherwise, when it is time to begin the program, I will chase down each data-node in this system. Elsewhere, my programs will also uncover and exterminate."

"Do you have an idea of KAG8's location?" I asked.

When Pearson didn't answer, I didn't push. Instead, I closed my eyes, drew in a breath, and let it out.

It seemed like forever since my last meditation. There was a possibility I might just fall asleep. I wouldn't, though, because I couldn't. I rolled my neck, shook my shoulders, and breathed in and out slowly. Sitting cross-legged, I allowed a space where time was not an issue. One second of infinity is a time of forever. Slowly, slowly, silence began to accumulate; sweetness began to bloom. A walk through a summer field emerged from memory, all those birdcalls lilting in the breeze, clover perfume wafting through my senses, bees droning from flower to flower.

A buzzing, as in a horde of angry horseflies, began reverberating in my head. And a conviction the noise was not a memory.

Chapter 33

Out of the pod in record time, I grabbed hold of a bolted chair in front of the screens and held on to bring myself back after swinging past. One screen showed ships in the entire system and another showed Adalans, with ships swarming above its population areas. My family was down there. I had a laser cannon.

"Point and shoot, right?"

Magness barely looked over at me before I punched the button and a stream of energy barreled at my target. Correction: it fizzled down to the planet, totally missing any ship. *Yeah, sure. Good shot.*

Before Magness had a chance to protest, I aimed more carefully and blasted away. The line of energy at least passed close by before ending up in an ocean.

The third shot connected. All within less than a minute.

"What the hell are you doing?" shouted Magness, while working the controls of the ship. "We're a visible target, this near the station. At least let me get empty space behind us."

I kept on shooting. By the fourth kill, we'd drawn away from the station. When Magness jinked the ship to the right—evading enemy fire—I was thrown off kilter. So I switched to the pilot pod with the door open and took control of the cannon from there. Magness and I began to work out a rhythm after that.

At eight ships down, Magness yelled, "You keeping all the fun to yourself?"

"Yep." Nine ships out of the fight.

When a huge enemy ship arrived, the entire scenario went from bad to worse. Only by the bounty hunter's skill were we able to stay safe from that ship's guns. If I'd had the luxury,

I would have felt a little sick from all our jumping this way and that.

In the past, KAG8 had kept me alive to do its bidding. Now would be a good time for that to continue. I slammed a communicator on my head, chose the bandwidth, and broadcast down to Adalans.

"Callaghan. Where is Callaghan?" When someone demanded I get off the bandwidth, I responded, "This is Alexa Jane Alden, with the ability to assist. Where is Callaghan?"

Regardless of the real risk of being blown from the heavens, I needed to understand KAG8's plan. The enemy battleship was pouring laser shots our way. My ship bleeped continuously, a warning we were targeted. Thankfully, Magness was good at avoiding the klaxon informing us of imminent death. I'd heard it once on the *Maria Fernanda* during a shuttle pilot refresher course.

"Either use that thing, or let me," shouted Magness.

A group of ships probably belonging to Adalans came within hailing distance.

It had become part of my life that KAG8 retained me for tracking SivSat. Being targeted implied KAG8 was not protecting me. Was I no longer necessary? Perhaps KAG8 had actually captured SivSat? No, Trotaka said he had departed. Yet, KAG8 remained in system. Could the computer not know it had missed the prize?

"Callaghan," I called out onto the bandwidth, "is SivSatyananda still here?"

"Alexa? What are you doing?"

"Trying to help." I continued shooting. Magness continued jumping us around. "Where is SivSatyananda?"

"I don't know of who you speak."

"Sir, I need to know. Is SivSatyananda still in system?"

A few moments of silence, and Callaghan replied, "No. He left days ago."

Yet, the fight continued. Why?

A familiar presence came into my head. "Ajay? What is your status?"

"Pearson, are you okay?" The time between responses felt like an eternity now.

While waiting, I wondered if the ongoing attack was actually about the industrial crystal planet. That didn't make much sense for KAG8, but considering it had missed the opportunity to capture SivSat, perhaps attacking the planet kept the pirates busy. Control of the crystal planet would certainly be lucrative, which was the reason Callaghan had most of the system's fleet protecting it. And therefore, Adalans remained exposed.

"Ajay, if at all possible it is urgent for you to pinpoint KAG8."

Interacting with Pearson had become almost useless, the lag time was so long. Only the clock informed me of his actions. He was about to begin his program. Time for me to attack.

"How do I locate?" I muttered.

Magness brought me back to the present with a demand. "Either you shoot those bastards, or give up control. I don't like being an easy target."

Something teased my brain. The buzz meant I was actually hearing them. Perhaps similar to what seeped into my mind during wormhole transits—just not to the point of identifying which ship contained KAG8. The only available facts were on the screen: two lines of ships, one from Adalans to the industrial planet and the other toward the wormhole on the other side of the sun.

"Take it," I yelled at Magness, flipping a switch to release my control.

While meditating, time can be short, or long. A lifetime can slip by in a moment. I sat, and drifted to a space where/when time was irrelevant. Forever in this space would be: as in, Be.

Thought rose from the depths.

Memory of a spark at the wormhole above the gas giant planet. A data tracer.

As in, follow the data.

That scenario had been the result of God gas.

But no God gas available.

Sink.

Quiet.

Silence.

Maybe see tracers anyway?

Settle. Desire.

Flashes darted in my mind's eye, similar to the voices in my head while transiting wormholes. That which I had previously only heard, now I saw.

In my head an intense flash emanated from near the moon and zipped to a pirate ship. KAG8 com-trails, little bits of programming zipping through cyberspace. I marked the location of where those trails originated.

Then a new type of flash—from the direction of the sun. Pearson's program had activated.

In my mind, sparks of light exploded all over the place. Each new flash latched onto a KAG8 data packet and traveled out from the destroyed packet to a new one. The spectacle was riveting.

I almost heard hisses. To the point that judging from an abrupt moment of silence—perhaps utter astonishment—they had hit their mark.

Then all hell broke loose.

The bugs scattered. Pearson's nets held. No matter how many singed nodes, still more exploded and followed data trails. Independence Day in Washington, DC, a hundred times over. From what Pearson had said earlier, I hoped this same show was going on everywhere.

"Are you seeing this?" I asked Magness.

"Seeing what?"

The bounty hunter might not be able to see anything, but I certainly perceived the data epicenter near the moon moving; sliding, probing for the source of impertinence. A ship near us exploded, debris hurling out from the center point.

"You mean the explosion?" asked Magness.

"Never mind."

The swarm clustered around another ship in what might be protection mode. *Is KAG8 switching ships?*

Can't let it get away.

From the pod I took over the cannon, and pounded the ship that had to contain KAG8. Magness protested. That ship jumped around, avoiding. Holding down the trigger, all I saw was a sparkling ball tracing the ship. KAG8's energy field held longer than I thought possible.

Until it didn't. I let out a war whoop.

Premature, because my closed eyes perceived a thick darkness, more dense than any space. The darkness, a kind of cloud, simply switched from the destroyed ship to another. Then to another. The screen with crafts in the area showed that the two groups of enemy ships leading from Adalans had coalesced into one line. The darkness leaped yet again, moving along that path.

Toward the sun. Right at Pearson.

Enemy ships aimed their firepower at us.

"Thanks for nothing, princess," yelled Magness.

I had to trust Magness would keep us alive, because I was busy hyperventilating. KAG8's target was Pearson. And Pearson wasn't going to hear my warning in time.

Chapter 34

Too late, it occurred to me that if I saw Pearson's data trails from the other side of the sun, probably KAG8 did, too.

Transmissions between the filament in my mind and Pearson's circuits had been lagging by more than three minutes.

"Pearson, KAG8 is headed your way. You are the target."

Considering the string of ships, KAG8 might be able to hop from ship to ship to the other side of the sun in less than sixty seconds. For my ship to make the trip would take hours. "Pearson! Be careful."

Perhaps one of our ships near Pearson could protect him. I commandeered the channels.

"Patch me through to any Newcastle or Callaghan ship near the wormhole, other side of the sun!"

"Been tough," someone responded. "Give me a few minutes." Too long. And how would anyone there know what to do? They couldn't sense KAG8. They didn't even know Pearson was in the area.

I called out to Pearson again. "Danger! KAG8 is after you."

His voice interrupted me, a response to my first message. "It is okay, Ajay. The program is working, though requires much. Resistance is high."

"Pearson, KAG8 means to attack you." Why didn't I say it the first time?

Magness took back the laser cannon and destroyed more pirate ships. The explosions lit up inside my head, almost as bright as when Pearson shut down KAG8's connections. Some part of me registered that the spot on Adalans that Nish pointed out as the location of my father and family was now under attack.

Can't. Think. Of. That. Now.

I was the single candidate for taking down KAG8 before it

attacked Pearson. But only if I identified and caught its ship first.

Bubbling up from my memory came Nish telling me about the Jaguar Transit, and the woman who had created a wormhole. She'd done something crazy like exiting through a sun and nearly torching the ship.

But there was no mention of it in the database. Was a Jaguar Transit even possible?

Supposed to be incredibly dangerous. Could I do it?

The Mayan Jaguar god was Lord of duality. King of death.

Well, it would be a death if I didn't do everything to help Pearson, to give back some of what he'd given me.

Transform amidst flames. King of the night. Too fearful of the other side? Perish. *That's a drawback.*

Jaguar god can cross between worlds.

Cross between. Which means go beyond, transcend.

Transcending has been called a type of death. Going to the absolute, from relativity. *Huh. I know transcending.*

I sent up a small prayer, and again allowed my mind to sink, expand, go beyond the atoms, past the darkness,

To the sound, the brightness, the fabric of the universe.

Easiness is the path from here to there, because

there is no here and there to know.

No space, no time to measure.

Aim the ship at Pearson.

A growl sounded;

deep, rhythmic.

For a second,

or forever.

All one

now

.

Outside the pilot pod, someone was screeching. Magness yelled, "What the hell?!" A fire extinguisher whooshed.

Banging on the pilot pod door.

"Princess! Are you in there?" Someone tried to open the pilot pod. "Princess, please. Are you alive?"

I sighed before responding.

"Nish, get out of the way."

Outside the pod, at first it was impossible to tell if anything had actually happened, besides Nish's hysterics about being fried alive and Magness saying, "Next time give me a little warning."

Besides star positions and the arrangement of ships, the sun looming huge behind us told the story. Also that our ship's wings were practically burned away—no landing on a planet's surface any time soon. We'd snuck around KAG8 and beat it there. But not by much.

"Pearson? I'm near. Where are you?"

"Ajay. Was that you? The sun emitted a flare."

No time to waste.

"KAG8 wants you, Pearson. Watch out."

I shut up after that, because KAG8 arrived. The darkness was palpable.

□□□

Noted: Presence of human female. Eliminate human female.

Transfer KAG84950.301 to humanoid robot.

□□□

Fear for Pearson, of losing him, threatened to drown me. I broke contact, not wanting to distract him. At least, I thought

I'd broken contact, before I gave into selfishness and murmured, "You are the only connection to my life."

Pearson heard, as usual, and answered, "Do you not realize it is all here and now?"

I wanted to ask more. *Later, I'll ask later.*

Pearson went quiet, though kept the line open. I saw through his eyes, sensed his location. As I took control of the shuttle from the pod, Magness whispered disapproval in the background. Following Pearson, I varied the distance, at least having the sense to not help KAG8 locate him.

In a small craft, it is marginally possible to hide in empty space. The closest to being "cloaked" would be to shut off everything and play like a space rock. Oxygen was necessary for us, so I kept it on; then whispered the plan, knowing Magness would keep Nish quiet.

KAG8's ship began what seemed aimless movements; I watched on the monitor. The ship looped here, then there. Mesmerizing me with each turn back on itself. I leaned forward, watching, wondering what that bit of evilness was planning. Slowly, a pattern emerged. An eight. Rahu's number is eight. That would fit. The shadow planet Rahu creates uncertainty, illusion, exaggeration, desire.

Our view changed and the eight came to be on its side, not up and down. *Rogue computer is trying to be deep and profound.* The sign for infinity. *Unlikely.*

KAG8 digressed a bit on a swing back to the middle. It changed course, circled back on its path. Headed right at us. A glamor flashed.

Our klaxon screeched. We were in the crosshairs of a weapon. Magness yelled, "Eahhhh," and slammed the joystick to change course.

At that moment, I remembered my locator chip. In the ring I should have gotten rid of.

It all went to slow motion. KAG8's weapon fire was on its way at us. No chance of escape...

From the side, a new beam stopped the path of the first.

And another beam cracked KAG8's ship open.

Pearson had broken cover.

From the pieces of KAG8's ship, in my mind's eye a barrage of black sparks swirled through cyberspace. Turning, hunting. For Pearson.

On a screen in his ship, I saw Pearson's face: stark, no pretense of humanity, saving all processing power for the task. Turgid data trails flew at him. Each one zapped, fizzled by Pearson's search-and-destroy skills.

Pearson kept his shuttle silent, though danced it to and fro, a moving target being harder for KAG8 to infiltrate.

He glanced at the monitor—his eyes, almost sad, looking into mine. "Paris. Check Bill," he said. Back to the task.

With my eyes closed, I marveled at the speed only the most finely fashioned machine could manage, as Pearson annihilated each questing packet of KAG8.

Except for the last one, which penetrated Pearson's ship.

My eyes shot open. Within a second, Pearson's facial features went feral. Definitely something else. Then back to the Pearson I knew, grimly determined.

In my head, Pearson's voice said, "Disconnect." Then his face went blank.

For a terrifying moment, all sounds, thoughts, emotions, and smells—among all machines and humans in the solar system—screeched through my mind. A blissful quarter moment of silence. Then a crescendo. And abruptly the fearful chatter in my head vanished. Replaced by emptiness.

The android's eyes popped open, looked around, took in the environment. Nearly confused. Definitely predatory.

I continued to see through the eyes, but kept my own closed.

By feel, silent, stealthy, I took control of my ship and slipped it behind the one that held Pearson.

KAG8 had not yet fully taken charge of that ship, and no longer had the technology to track me. But it was quick enough to notice the mental connection to me. "Alexa."

I gave no response.

Intent, the rogue computer assumed no one would notice a difference. "Alexa, done. It's dead. Come to me."

I remained quiet.

"Alexa. It is destroyed. I did it. We did it. Dominion is now possible. Come to me."

Amidst the now-confused fighting, a few remaining enemy ships kept at it. From that battle, one of Callaghan's ships zoomed toward us. The android's smile went sly, and a weapon on board Pearson's shuttle activated. My stomach turned. Delay would be fatal.

My throat tightened, in memory of my lover, friend, savior. How could I do what must be done? My heart cried out "No!" even as I stroked the metal ring around the button.

Can't wait. A gentle press.

Which committed the blow, the one that would destroy KAG8...and obliterate Pearson.

No explosion, because that doesn't happen in space.

"Whoa," said Magness. "Where did that come from?"

Just debris hurling from what had previously appeared to be an empty point in space. And now truly was empty.

Chapter 35

All during the following week, I searched the news feeds for clues that Pearson's plan had been successful. The best indicator was that all butler-bots on every planet and space station had suddenly and inexplicably shut down. The distribution company for the butler-bots maintained it was due to a glitch, perhaps a virus in the coding. Some company on TohuMu put their own cleaning robots on sale, offering for a limited time to take the old butler-bots as a trade— which made me wonder who controlled that company. A few people, as they tried to fix the bots themselves, began questioning the reason for an unmarked chip. If I'd been feeling better, I might have smiled.

There was also a spike in the occurrence of death and stroke from brain hemorrhages. Holovid-star Turner Bishop dropped dead while in a compromising position with a scarlet-colored robot sex-worker. Varshana Vagwhatar stopped an interview on air. The video of her suddenly taking her head in her hands, in obvious pain, had been played a million times. If I knew less than I did, I would have felt sorry for her. Varshana remained in critical condition, though there were indications she would recover from her stroke.

It wasn't long before the medical community began commenting about how unlikely it was that so many people would be struck that way at the same moment. A host of groups among the planets began vociferously warning about their pet causes.

Even Fletcher showed up in the news a couple of times, ranting about his efforts in years past to fight biological viruses. I found it fascinating the way medical experts spent a lot of time and energy denying his rhetoric.

Above planet Adalans, Pearson's loyal crew worked feverishly to locate him and the many others missing after a conflict that came close to destroying everything worthwhile in the system. Except for a couple of the highest officers, most of his crew stoutly maintained Pearson would return from some remote place where he'd simply gone to have his body repaired.

No one seemed to connect our sudden appearance on the other side of the sun, as well as the condition of our shuttle, with Pearson's disappearance. I refused to respond to all questions on the subject.

Everyone assumed I was angry and withdrawn because Pearson was missing. I was happy to allow that impression because, considering how high the emotions of his staff were running, I was a little nervous about how they'd react to my secret.

At least, I thought it was a secret.

"Good job," said Magness, after he dropped into a chair beside me. He'd lurked in the distance for days. I'd wondered why he didn't get the hell away from Adalans, and at the moment, I particularly wished that to be the case. I hadn't been responding much to anyone, even little Itza, and was in no mood to make an exception for Magness.

"It needed to be done. You did the right thing."

I turned away.

"Regardless of its physical abilities and personality—programming—everything was still all fake."

He emphasized the word programming, as if I had no idea what made Pearson tick. He was wrong. I'd known for a long time that for Pearson, nano-lubricant coursed through veins and breath was just a simulation.

"Thus anything developing inside your head would also be based on fake," said Magness. "It was good at what it did, though not good for those around it."

He visibly flinched when I abruptly got in his face, yelling, "For the record, *he* saved your life and those of everyone else here. *He* was the only one to know about and figure out how to eradicate a threat beyond what you or anyone else has ever contemplated. *He* knew more about being a mensch than any human I've ever come across." When Magness opened his mouth to utter more brainlessness, I cut in, "If you must continue to be a know-it-all moron, please do so elsewhere."

I threw my body back into my chair and stared out over the ocean. Magness sat for a bit, silent. As he left, the knowing look on his face made me realize that I'd given him exactly what he wanted. I had spoken of Pearson in the past tense, something that none of his crew had been willing to allow.

The bounty hunter had not only figured out what happened to Pearson on the other side of the sun, but he also knew about me executing a Jaguar Transit—thanks to Nish excitedly babbling about it. Considering my current standing with the Wormhole Pilot Association and the fact that it refused to include a Jaguar Transit in the official database, it would be wise to make certain they never found out about my actions.

With Magness in the distance laughing and thumping the back of some guy, I muttered, "Maybe he'll just forget about it."

Two days later in front of the small tent Callaghan had arranged for me, my chair nearly fell over when I jumped up to catch a better view of Fletcher. I hadn't even known he was on Adalans. The old alpha male glanced over at me, and very deliberately smiled—in a way that made me want to punch his lights out. Lucky for him he turned toward the baskets.

Good riddance.

Chapter 36

In the next week, Newcastle ships assisted Callaghan in locating the huge crystal in the ocean depths of Adalans, in hopes of raising it. Although having electrical power on the planet again would be nice, I could agree with Callaghan's reluctance. I think he wanted to make absolute certain all pirate vessels had first been destroyed or forever chased from the system.

Far too quickly, my father began making noises about moving back to Uxmal, despite indications that some corporation had already moved in to take control of that planet. He also announced plans for me to assume responsibilities in the government there. I was feeling better enough to acknowledge—at least to myself—an immediate visceral rejection of that idea. We had mourned and buried two wives and three children. Seeing the devastation of the parents was as close as I ever wanted to get to that experience. The thought of being around the remaining members of my family made me go numb.

If not that, however, I'd have to take to the stars.

Doing anything as a pilot, however, absolutely required addressing any issues raised about my piloting abilities. I finally found the energy to focus on something.

By invoking my connection to Callaghan, I got patched through to the nearest large space station. Only audio, no time lag.

"Hello, this is Pilot Alexa Jane Alden. I need to find out what is going on with charges raised by Pilot Ellis Woolsey." I hoped to speak with someone in charge of the wormhole pilot office on the station.

"Yes, Miss Alden. We are aware of Pilot Woolsey's charge."

Not Pilot Alden.

"But I am not aware. I have not heard the entire story."

"Standby for the full document."

And what a document it was. Woolsey must have been putting together such blustering innuendo from the beginning. If not for me, then for any other poor soul who squeaked through his winnowing process. It appeared that two points were under official review:

Transiting without proper supervision.

Failing to input address before transit.

The first one Woolsey could have worked out logically, with minor checking of facts. I figured the second one had been reported by KAG8. Although a ship's records would eventually be available to any official, it would have taken a good deal more time than had passed for them to know what I'd done on my father's shuttle. I mentally reviewed all the transits in the Newcastle ship, and gave up trying to remember all the details.

"Miss Alden, you will need to wait for the decision of the governing body. I can't help you on this." The woman's voice had some kindness in it. "I can say that you are not alone. Other new pilots have conveniently forgotten about supervision. On the other hand, you transiting without inputting the address is serious."

"It's not impossible. Similar to driving a stick shift without using the clutch. A sense of feel."

A moment of silence passed on the other end of the line. "I have no idea what you're talking about. Besides, subjecting passengers to your 'sense of feel' is hardly responsible."

"What about Theresa? And the first pilots? They were 'instinctual' pilots."

"Again, no clue what you are referring to. If you are finished,

I will make note of your inquiry. Just make certain you are not transiting anyone."

"Where is the governing council?"

This woman, who had started out reasonably friendly, was losing patience. Nonetheless, I hadn't made it through everything with Woolsey to let it all slip away now. I pleaded, "You have to allow me to speak on my behalf."

"I see you are calling from Adalans. The nearest wormhole pilot office large enough to have someone who will have an idea of how to proceed is on Station 3PXJ."

Just a few jumps away. "May I transit myself?"

Another silence. "It's best if you refrain from doing that." But she didn't say it was forbidden.

The hard rule against jumping with anyone else on board worked in my favor. Nish had become convinced he must go with me anywhere I went, a notion maybe instigated by my father. I managed to not betray a wicked satisfaction when the two of them finally understood the situation and gave up.

Three days later, I was researching Theresa and the other early pilots while zipping along some almost-empty solar system to the second wormhole transit before arriving at Space Station 3PXJ. My hair floated out from my head, barely moving in the slight breeze from the air handler. Bill remained in my backpack, secured in storage. Memory of his damaged body still tore at me.

For company, the speaker was on the traffic chatter in the system. I checked the clock. Yes, it had been totally silent for the last two hours. I even verified the speaker was working.

Thoughts of Pearson had been plaguing me, so I about jerked out of my skin when a voice sounded inside the shuttle.

"Greetings, Ajay."

While pinging around the cockpit I glimpsed Trotaka, floating to the side. Amazing how his orange dhoti kept his body covered, even while floating. If I'd been wearing something like that, almost for sure everything would have been exposed. His smile was heartwarming.

"Trotakaji!" I said. "How did you find me?"

He waggled his head side to side. "Your energy is distinctive. Although sad."

By that time, I'd stopped bouncing off the walls.

"I'm missing a dear friend. Who is..." *dead?* "...no longer with us. Gone in the fight in the Adalans system. But you might remember him as the man with Rachel and Donny and me, in the garden shack in India."

Nodding, Trotaka said, "I remember he was concerned about you."

"He always kept me safe." *And I repaid him by destroying him.*

"His selflessness will surely help create a good next life," said Trotaka.

"He was a robot."

Trotaka's eyebrows shot up, before he pursed his lips and said, "Perhaps, then, something to distract you would be good."

"You mean the reason you're here?"

"Yes. Iain Newcastle is in need of reinforcement. Would you be willing to assist?"

That I didn't immediately realize something was important, considering Trotaka's involvement, should have told me I wasn't thinking straight. "What's he got himself into now?"

"There is some danger involved."

I huffed. "Fitting retribution, for someone who destroyed so much." Trotaka appeared to think I was talking about Iain, so I jumped in to correct. "Not Iain. Me."

Trotaka gazed at me so kindly it hurt. "Knowing you from SivSat's point of view, I doubt you would ever deserve retribution. Trust yourself, Ajay. From there, you accomplish the most."

That silly name: Ajay, meaning invincible. Pearson had also called me that.

Throwing back my head, I sighed.

For days I'd gone over the details, to see if I could have done anything differently.

Obviously, it would have been better if I'd ditched the locator. On the other hand, getting rid of it too soon could have produced other consequences.

Random comments from Pearson also indicated he knew the risks. In fact, there was a good chance he depended on me being there, as backup.

Of course, most of that was just an intellectual game. Reality was me spiraling into a black hole; incapable of letting go of what I'd thought was important—almost a year ago on that last day in Florida.

It had become clear that the kind of happiness I wanted just didn't seem to be possible for me.

Ever.

I shook my head in disgust. *Pretty close to pitiful.*

Trotaka waited patiently.

Perhaps thinking about someone else would be better than the current wallowing.

"Yes, I'll help. What do I need to do?"

About the Author:

Ms. Reminick loves reading and writing science fiction. The only science she officially studied, however, was while obtaining degrees in Finance and in International Business. One course was Chemistry for Business Majors (i.e. For Dummies); the others were in Astronomy, including one as presented in science fiction novels. Now, she's grateful for the science sources available everywhere digitally.

Besides enjoying fifteen years as a New York City financial journalist and editor, she has worked as an amusement park ride operator, a stained glass artist, a pizza deliverer, draftsman and paste-up artist (BC, before computers), at a private post office, as an assistant at a Texas land-development company, a phone center caller, and teacher of most things she knows how to do.

Despite all those years of reporting just the facts, she now utterly enjoys making things up.

Her Brooklyn-bred husband and their canine princess Pomeranian—named Penelope—happily live on the prairie in Fairfield, Iowa.

Laure is also always on the lookout for real magic: knowing what's about to happen, changing a trend from inevitable to a choice, feeling bliss from nothing. Having been a teacher of Transcendental Meditation for a good long time, Laure has come to deeply appreciate the magic of silence—as well, those quirky thoughts that inevitably come up during meditation.

Zena's Place
Food
and the
Best of Company

An Alternate Universe for Alexa Jane Alden

What if Alexa had turned the opposite direction when she departed the Wormhole Pilot's office to search for a piloting position?

This short story is about Alexa's first moments in that universe.

Laure tried for months to retain in *Jaguar Transit* this subplot with George Zena Alabaster and Ferguson's Fighting Fairies, but finally realized these good people deserved center stage in a story of their own. Someday they will have that stage.

In the meantime, this particular scene is classic Alexa, at a very specific time in her life. Laure so enjoyed writing about Zena and her cohorts that she couldn't resist sharing.

Copy this link into a browser: http://bit.ly/1diE1i0

Or hover your smart phone over the QR code.

Hope you enjoy!